MW01254907

Stories From The Creekbank

By

Curt Iles

I

To order copies or contact the author:
Creekbank Stories
PO Box 332
Dry Creek, LA 70637
Curtiles@aol.com

Other titles by Curt Iles:
Hearts across the Water (2005)
Wind in the Pines (2204)
The Old House (2002)
The Mockingbird's Song (2007)

Available on audio CD:
Hearts across the Water
Wind in the Pines
Old House Stories

Creekbank Stories exists to connect people's
hearts to God through stories.
Be sure to visit our website and blog page at
www.creekbank.net.

Acknowledgments

When I was seventeen my Uncle Bill bought me a blank notebook and simply said, "Begin a journal telling, in your own words about your life." This book is simply an outgrowth of that first journal. It contains the scribblings of my heart. Thanks Bill.

I am the world's worst proofreader but I've been helped by many folks on these stories. I'd especially like to thank Janet Bogard, Debra Tyler, and Glenda Hagan for their kind and patient input.

Most importantly I want to thank my sweet wife, DeDe, for tirelessly reading my stories, giving me input and supplying the encouragement to make this dream come true.

Dedication

Stories from the Creekbank is dedicated to the sweet memory of Brad Robinson. Brad was a special son in the Lord to me. He loved Dry Creek just as much as me. He will always be remembered as long as I can write.

Table of Contents

Book Three: Postcards from Dry Creek

Introduction

I once heard someone say we should try to see God in every grain of sand. I've tried to follow that belief in my life. I truly believe we stumble through this journey called life missing, or taking for granted, the wonderful gifts God gives us daily. Stories from the Creekbank is simply a compilation of how I've seen God's goodness in the things and people around me.

You'll notice that I do poke fun at many people in my stories. Just remember two things: I only laugh at my friends. So if you're in these stories, I value you as a friend. Secondly, if you will read carefully, you'll see that there is one person who gets the needle of humor stuck in him more than anyone else. His name is Curt Iles.

X

Book One:
Stories from Dry Creek

Curt Iles

Prologue

Dry Creek, Louisiana is off the beaten path and that's fine with me. It's a place way behind the rest of the world and that is what makes it so special. Located in the piney woods of southwestern Louisiana, it is unincorporated, uncluttered, and the place I call home.

Chapter One

The Evening Holler

I sit in the woods on a cold still October morning. I love this time of year when the weather becomes cool and the sky is usually clear. I also like the beginning and end of each day as the sun rises or sets. As daybreak comes across Crooked Bayou swamp, it is so still and quiet. A mile through the woods I hear a neighbor's roosters crowing. In another direction I hear my brother in law's loud voice scolding a dog. I'm always amazed at how sound carries so clearly and distinctly in the woods.

As it gets quiet again and I shift on my deer stand, a lone owl gives his eight note song. Soon he is joined by another sentinel way across the swamp. These two barred owls converse back and forth in their unique eight note call:

"Hoo hoo-hoo hoo,   hoo hoo-hoo hoawww"

Always when I hear this owl I recall old-timers describing his call as,

"Who cooks for you?   Who cooks for you?"

Even when you know it's an owl there's something spooky about his eerie cry. As I listen to them, I'm drawn back to one of my favorite stories of the settling of our community.

Always when I hear those far off sounds in the woods, I recall the story of "The Evening Holler." My great grandparents, Frank and Dosia Iles, told me of this event. This unique call, a tradition going back to the pre-Civil War

5

settling of the Dry Creek area, was a primitive means of communication among these early settlers.

The first white settlers in Dry Creek lived in the woods along the creeks and streams. They were surrounded by vast tracts of pine forests. This area of Southwestern Louisiana was a neutral strip claimed by both Spain and the United States. There was no law. Later on when there was law, the nearest officer was in Opelousas over seventy miles away. Indians, though friendly, stilled roamed the woods. Bears and mountain lions were common in the swamps.

Because these pioneers were homesteading tracts of land, they seldom built homes right next to each other. They were forced by necessity to depend on each other. So they developed an ingenious method of checking on the welfare of neighbors. Late in the evening at dusk, each man would stand in the yard or on the porch of his home. Just as the sun dropped behind the wooded horizon, the ritual would begin.

Each man would begin hollering his own individual yell. Each of the pioneers had his own unique hollering style-easily recognized by his own pitch and voice. The closest neighbor would answer back. He would be joined by the next neighbor down the creek. As the evening holler passed down through the woods, each man would then be assured as to the well-being of his neighbor as he heard an answering yell in return.

In spite of the distance between home places, the hollering carried for long distances. Remember, this was a time before televisions, air conditioners, or vehicles. There were fewer artificial sounds to drown out the evening noises. If you've ever really been out in the woods, you'll understand what we mean when we call it "an eerie silence."

My ancestors told me of how if a man did not hear the call of his neighbor, he would holler several more times at different intervals. If he still did not receive a reply, he'd go check on his neighbor. My great-grandmother told of seeing her father saddle up his horse to go check on a neighbor who did not answer. Even though things were usually fine at the neighbors, he went each time to double check. To him it was simply a matter of being a good neighbor. These early settlers took care of each other. The evening holler was kind of an early version of today's Neighborhood watch.

Sometimes when I'm enjoying the quietness of a fall sunset, I'll hear the owls begin calling to each other across the woods. Or in April, I'll listen to the whip-poor-wills as they answer each other with their own version of the evening holler. It's at times like this that I think about the evening holler and what it meant . . .

It reminds me of how our ancestors took care of each other. They truly considered a neighbor . . . a neighbor. In our modern busy crowded life, we seldom know our neighbors-much less check on their well-being. Even with all of our marvelous modern communication tools from telephones to fax machines to e-mail, we usually know much less about our neighbors than our ancestors did.

As I sit here thinking about these things and how much we've lost in "neighborliness.", my neighbor drives by in his truck. He honks as he sees me sitting on the porch. His truck is loaded with firewood. All fall and into winter, he cuts firewood for the widows and needy of our community. He's on his way with a load to give someone right now. Then the thought hits me: maybe the evening holler is not as dead an art as I think it is.

Then I recall another neighbor who daily checks on an elderly woman who lives alone. He makes time to take care of this person. Then I think of my parents who've always picked up the mail for another home-bound senior adult. I then remember the times, when after a house fire in our community, people have banded together to supply needed items and volunteer to help rebuild the home. I recall the time-honored Southern tradition of supplying food to families who've had a death.

As I think of each of these, and many more I could name, I realize how much good and caring there still is in people.

Yes, times have changed. We don't live in as close contact with our neighbors as we should. As humans we need to take ownership on the care of our neighbors. It is a decision that each of us can choose to do. It is a positive decision that many of my community neighbors have chosen to do. As I take time to really look, I still see the spirit of the evening holler alive and well in a small community I love called Dry Creek.

Chapter Two

A Pair for Life

Clay, Clint, and I crawled over the wet leaves to the bluff bank on the small stream called Dry Creek. We were just west of where the creek runs into Bundick Creek. As we crawled along, I kept looking at the boys reminding them to stay quiet because I knew I'd heard wood ducks on the creek...

As we slid along up to the cliff edge, we saw them a male drake resplendent in the beautiful colors that make the wood duck my favorite bird. He was swimming along beside his drab colored hen companion. They were aware of something being wrong but couldn't quite place where we were as they nervously swam in circles.

It was a special moment in my life one of my sons on each side lying on the high bank as we watched the pair of ducks swimming about.

The boys kept looking back at my shotgun which was leaning against a nearby tree. I kept shaking my head no when they imploringly looked at me. We lay there about 10 minutes just enjoying watching them. Eventually the ducks swam down Dry Creek and out into the stronger current of Bundick... and then they were gone.

My sons upbraided me pretty bad about not shooting the ducks. I tried to explain that they were a pair. If my understanding of waterfowl was correct, they were a couple just the same and me and their mom. I just didn't have the heart to shoot. I'm not sure the boys understood, but one day they probably will.

I thought about that pair of ducks when we buried my Grandmother. As I sat with my Grandfather at the hospital before her death and then was with him at the funeral, my mind kept returning to those two ducks in the creek a pair for life.

Grandpa and Grandma Sid, as we called them, were married over 62 years when she died. Throughout my memory, they only existed together... inseparable. During my childhood I always looked forward to their visits. I recalled summer weeks spent in Shreveport with them. Whenever and wherever I saw them, they were together My Grandpa and Grandma Sid.

Now as I thought about it, they were no longer together. How it hurt my heart to see him alone. How lonely it must have been after spending practically every moment together over the last twenty years and sharing life together for over sixty.

I thought about my own wife, DeDe, and how close we are. And I thought about the loneliness one of us will one day endure. And once again I could see the wood ducks swimming off together... and it occurred to me how long 62 years must be and how quickly 62 years must seem to pass. Then my grandfather's words came back to me, "Well, if I'd had her 92 years, I still wouldn't have wanted to have given her up."

There are so many things I don't understand about life. Life is full of so much happiness and sadness. We live and love the same person for a lifetime of happiness, in this case 62 years worth, and then it must end sadly - and alone.

There is so much we just don't understand but we must choose. We can concentrate on the happy memories and joy shared together... the intertwining of two lives wrapped together by love. Or we can dwell on the sorrow and loneliness that comes to us when "death does up part."

I choose to think about those two happy wood ducks swimming off into the current together... and those wonderful memories of my grandparents together.

Chapter Three

One Step at a Time

I grew up on a one-mile stretch of gravel road in Dry Creek. Our house was the only house at the dead end of this narrow country lane. My dad always said when he heard a car coming down the road, "Well, they're either coming to see us . . . or they're lost."

This hilly Louisiana road was lined with pine forests on each side. As a young boy, I spent many hours walking and riding my bicycle on this road. Later, as a teenager, I would take night time walks on this road. As I walked under the stars, the only sounds would be the crunching of gravel underfoot, the sound of the wind in the pines, and other nighttime noises- crickets chirping, frogs singing, and occasionally the cry of geese flying overhead.

My nighttime walks were times of solitude. As I'd look up into the clear night sky, thousands of stars would be visible. As I'd gaze at the vast field of glittering stars, one thought always hit me,

"How can anyone not believe in God when they look into the night sky?"

Many times I took my night time walk to mull over a decision or pray about a problem. One particular instance still stands out in my mind . . .

During my first three semesters of college I had not declared a major. I was yet unsure of what career decision to make. I'd reached the point where I must choose an area of concentration. I knew this was a life-determining decision. As a 19-year-old young man, I was scared by the magnitude of this decision. I felt as if I was standing on a road with several forks in the pathway ahead. I must choose one direction to go. I also wanted God's will in my life.

11

If only He would show me . . . I was willing to go in that direction.

So during my Christmas holidays home, I found myself walking down the gravel road, thinking about this decision. It was a cold and clear winter night as I walked along. The stars shone brightly as they only can on a clear moonless clear country night. As I walked along in the dark only the starlight lit my path. Each step was a step of faith due to the extreme darkness.

As I walked I prayed about my career decision,

"Lord guide me. Show me what to do."

Then in the quietness of the moment God spoke to me. Not in an audible voice, but deep down in my heart- right where He speaks to all of us. What I heard in my heart was this:

As you walk down this gravel road, you cannot see to the end of it. However, by taking one step at a time in the darkness, you will reach the end. There is just enough light for each step- no more, no less.

I then realized that God was not going to lay out His plan for my entire life or even for the next five years. He instead wisely chose to lead me step by step . . . moment by moment. My responsibility was simply to take it one step at a time in the light I had. I didn't have to see all the way to the end of the road to take one step. God knew my life's road all of the way to the end. He would guide me without fail.

This "enlightening" experience on a dark gravel road helped guide the decisions I needed to make as a 19-year old. More than 20 years later, God still is, when I listen, willing to give the guidance

I need . . . *One step at a time.*

Even though I no longer live on that long gravel road, I still take night time walks. As I walk outside and my eyes adjust to the darkness, I'm still amazed by the beautiful handiwork

God has placed in the night sky. I often find myself saying, "Lord, you've really outdone yourself tonight." But even more amazing than the vast number of stars is the fact that out of billions of people, He still has time to direct my steps . . . *One step at a time.*

Chapter Four

The Wall

...By my God have I leaped over a wall.   Psalms 18:29

As I stood in the shadow of the twelve-foot wall, sweat popped out on my forehead. In my ears rang the screaming chants of more than fifty teenagers:

"Curt!"   "Curt!"   "Curt!"

I knew I was in a bind. There was no graceful way to avoid going over the wall. What had started out as an enjoyable tour of the camp grounds had turned into a living nightmare for me! In front of this large group of teenagers and their adult leaders I knew I couldn't back down.

As we'd approached the wall on our adventure recreation course, Billy Gibbs had loudly announced, "Don't you all want to see our new camp manager go over the wall?" With that the chant began . . . I felt like a scared challenger in the boxing ring with a heavyweight champion. (Once when Joe Louis was preparing to fight a boxer who was prone to evade contact instead of fight, Louis stated, "He can run but he can't hide.")

Well, I could run . . . and for a brief instant I even considered it, but I couldn't hide. I mean I'm the camp manager- I couldn't embarrass myself in front of these people. You see, my problem was this- I'm scared of high places. They call it "Acrophobia" and I've got a good dose of it. If you get me above the third rung on a ladder, my legs get wobbly. I try my best to stay right down on solid earth. I always think of the preacher who was scared of heights, and especially airplanes, who justified this fear with scripture: *"And **lo**, I am with you always."*

But here I was standing at the wall . . . and I had no scripture to excuse myself. I knew I was going over whether I was willing or not. So I did what I could to make the best of a bad situation. Nearby stood our youth director, Kevin Willis. So I called my best shot. "If Kevin will go up first, I'll go next."

As I looked at Kevin, a big robust forester weighing more than 220 pounds, I felt better about going over the wall. I knew how strong Kevin was. (I'd been bear hugged enough by him at church to know his strength.) I had faith Kevin wouldn't drop me on my trip over the wall.

So we all gathered around and boosted Kevin up the wall. As I helped shove, the sound of Kevin's tennis shoes sliding against the wooden wall above my head reminded me of how high twelve feet really is.

Then Kevin was straddling the top of the wall. Now it was my turn. I took my wristwatch off . . . I thought about telling someone to give it to my wife if I didn't make it. Then I thought better and put it in the pocket of my jeans.

With a surge they pushed me up . . . Kevin grasped my right wrist in a strong vise-like grip and pulled me upwards. With my left hand I pulled myself up onto the top of the wall. It was definitely too late to turn back now.

The height was dizzying but it wasn't as bad as I'd imagined. And in place of the knot of fear in my stomach, a strong jolt of adrenaline told me: "You've done it! You're on the wall!" A feeling of accomplishment burned in my heart . . . The same heart that was beating wildly due to the fear, exhilaration, and the physical effort required to get on top of the wall.

But I was quickly jolted back to reality by the sound of yelling down on the ground:

"Who's next to volunteer?"

To my amazement the first volunteer (I wouldn't call

15

Kevin or myself "volunteers") was the only person I knew
more afraid of heights than me . . . There standing at the
bottom, arms raised to be pulled up, was my 11-year old son,
Clay. I couldn't believe he was willing to do this. He hated
high places worse than I.

They quickly pushed Clay up. I'll always remember
how tightly I grabbed his wrist when he came up. Right
behind him came his younger brother, Clint. After these two,
a whole host of squealing, giggling, and squirming teenagers
came over the wall. Kevin and I carefully helped each one
up and over.

As I climbed down the wall, it was a special feeling
to have accomplished something so difficult for me. As I
looked at the wall, it no longer seemed as high as it once did.
In the past it had loomed as largely as Mount Everest. Once
scaled, it was reduced in my mind to its actual size.

Then I stopped to think about the spiritual lessons of the
wall. Many of life's problems look insurmountable from
ground level. Only when we attack them, and succeed, do
we then realize the problem was not as big as we'd made it
look in our mind.

Just as the wall represents life's problems, those who
boosted me over the wall remind me of people who help us
in life. None of us can make it in life without the assistance
of friends. I am so thankful for the many friends who've
"boosted me" when I needed it.

I trusted Kevin Willis, partly because of how strong
he was, but mainly because he was my friend. To make it
in life, we must trust and depend on others. As my mom
always said, "You can't have too many friends." None of us
can make it on our own.

Then my sons had trusted me . . . I was their father.
Being up there above them, they knew my grip was sure and
firm. Nothing could happen to them while in their father's

hands. Isn't that a beautiful picture of just how our Heavenly Father is? When we are in His hands, we need not worry about being dropped. Wherever we go, and regardless of what happens to us, we are safely held by Him.

And Jesus said, ". . . *No man is able to pluck them out of my Father's hand.*" John 10:29

Chapter Five

Christmas Jelly

Of all my Christmas memories and traditions, Christmas jelly is one of my favorites. Each year I receive this special gift from a very special lady in my life. Before I share what Christmas jelly is, let me share about the special person who gives it to me each year.

Eleanor Andrews is my neighbor in Dry Creek. For all of my life she has lived in the same house along Highway 113. Her house is easy to spot across the highway from the camp. It has the prettiest yard in our community. Her beautiful garden, flowers, and shrubs are examples of her love of gardening.

But Mrs. Andrews is more than just my neighbor and a lover of flowers. She is also my all-time favorite teacher. Mrs. Andrews taught fifth grade at Dry Creek High School and later at East Beauregard High. She taught practically every young person in Dry Creek for a period of a quarter century.

Now Eleanor Andrews was from the "Old school." She was stern and took no gruff or lip off any student. Everything was rigid and "down the line" in her classroom. In her class there was no doubt that she was captain of the ship. She possessed a stare (made complete with her tongue tucked firmly in her cheek) that would stop a charging grizzly bear in its tracks.

Her reputation preceded her . . . And she was just as strict as the older kids on the bus had described her to be when I sat in her fifth grade class. But I also saw something else: Beneath that gruff exterior were warm smiling eyes. She loved watching students learn and leading young people to new knowledge. During that year, 1967, she became my favorite teacher. And now thirty years later, she still is.

Now let me get back to that Christmas jelly . . . Eleanor Andrews has been retired for many years and is much older and frailer than when she ruled the fifth grade at East Beauregard. Because of her health she doesn't venture out much anymore. She lives alone in her house surrounded by her flowers and memories of a life filled with teaching and touching lives.

Each year a few weeks before Christmas I receive a phone call from Mrs. Andrews. She tells me "to drop by her house." I know that the best Christmas present of the season is now complete- Christmas jelly is ready.

Before going I cut one of the Christmas trees from my farm. I've already tagged it weeks earlier. I have carefully chosen one that will meet her exacting standards. After loading this tree in my truck, I nervously drive to her home. I hope she will approve of my tree. Once again I feel as if I'm in the fifth grade waiting to hand in an important assignment.

As I enter her living room, she greets me with that special smile I've known over the years. Always when I'm in her presence she makes me feel as if I'm the most important person in the world- That's why she's always been my favorite teacher.

Into my arms she thrusts a basket of eight jars- all filled with homemade jelly. There are all of my favorites-muscadine, mayhall, even crabapple! Included are several jars of hot pepper jelly, and to top it all off, a Ziploc bag of chocolate "Martha Washington's" sits on top of the basket.

I look at this assortment of homemade jelly and my mouth waters thinking about all the biscuits it will top off during the coming year. Oh, the joys of homemade jelly! As Mrs. Andrews happily examines her Christmas tree, she insists on paying for it. Laughing I say, "No way, the best

19

deal I ever make each year is trading a tree for the best home-made jelly in Dry Creek."

After we visit for a while, I leave with my arm load of jelly jars. As I get in my truck, I think about the art of giving. Emerson said it well when he stated, "The only true gift is a portion of yourself." As I look at the colorful decorated jars of jelly, I'm once again reminded of what Christmas is truly about. It is all about giving- Giving of ourselves and sharing what we have. I'm so glad to live in a place where gifts such as Christmas jelly abound.

P.S. One of the things I appreciate about our kitchen crew at Dry Creek Camp is how they take a meal to Mrs. Andrews each time we serve a meal. This was started by Rea Tate and is carried on now by Betty Harper, Linda Farmer, and all of our cooks

Several weeks ago I took our youth group to visit Mrs. Andrews on a Sunday evening. I told each teenager to introduce themselves and tell who their parents are. It was so special to see the look on her face . . . and theirs . . . as she told how she'd taught their dad or mom. "Why you look just like your dad did in high school!" Of the 15 youth, she'd taught practically every one of their parents!

Chapter Six

A Dead Tree with Deep Roots

This morning I went by to check on one of my favorite trees in the whole world. As my youngest son Terry and I left our deer stand deep in Crooked Bayou Swamp, we made a detour through the woods. As we walked under the towering oaks and hickories, a late fall was at its colorful height on the day after Thanksgiving.

In a few minutes we came up on it: A huge beech tree standing by itself. All around it lay dead limbs that had fallen from its heights. All that now stands is the huge trunk and a few large limbs. This was my first trip by it this hunting season and I was shocked at how much it had deteriorated since last year. As I looked at it I wondered if this was the last year it would withstand the blowing winds of winter.

Even with its rotting condition I could still point out to Terry what made this beech so special. There about six foot high was carved:

F.I.

L.I.

10/9/21

"F.I". was my great grandfather, Frank Iles, and "L.I". was my grandfather, Lloyd Iles. On a hunting trip of their own over seventy-six years ago, they had stopped and carved in this tree. On that day my great-grandfather was thirty-six and his son was ten. I would estimate that this old beech tree is now well over one hundred years old.

On this day in 1997 my son and I are close to the respective ages of my beloved ancestors. As we stand looking at this tree, the sense of my deep roots once again overwhelms me. How special it is to stand on land that has been in my family for over one hundred years.

But another emotion also overwhelms me. The feeling of how quickly life passes by.

Each time I stand at this tree and see how it is slowly, but steadily dying, I am reminded of the surety of life passing rapidly by right before our eyes. When I bring one of the boys to this special place in the woods, they invariably ask, "Now, who was Frank Iles? And who was Lloyd Iles?" They don't know them as "Pa" and "PaPa", the beloved guides of my first eleven years of life.

Then I realize that one day someone will stand in these same woods by a tree where I've carved my initials. And one of my descendants will try to explain who "C.I." was...

Yes, time passes by so quickly... and the limbs of life fall to the ground as sure as the wind blows cold in November. What precious gifts we have been given: the gift of life, the wonderful gift of family- both past and present, and the gift of an old beech tree deep in Crooked Bayou swamp.

Chapter Seven

Bro. Hodges' Best Sermon

Kenneth Hodges was my pastor as a teenager. How can I begin to describe him? He was probably one of the countriest-looking men I've ever known. . . Tall and skinny with a large adam's apple and a shock of wavy black hair, Bro. Hodges was just really down to earth . . . and that is why everyone in Dry Creek loved him. He was a "what you see is what you get" kind of guy.

But his physical appearance is not what made him special. It was his loving spirit and kindness toward everyone. When he became pastor of Dry Creek Baptist Church in the early 1970's, he soon became "the pastor" to everyone in our community- whether they were church-goers or not. He had great rapport with all types of people.

Because he and his family lived in the old church parsonage on the camp grounds (located west of the dining hall) Bro. Hodges was always involved in all aspects of Dry Creek Camp. I fondly recall his family dropping in at meal time to help serve, visit, and eat with the staff.

Bro. Hodges was a very good preacher . . . But what he did best was "pastor." He cared about people and it showed daily. I've always believed the following story is his "best sermon":

One Monday Bro. Hodges dressed up in his best suit. I can still see it- A white leisure suit with blue stitching and buttons and white patent leather shoes. I always told him he looked like the Easter bunny when he wore it. He was going "into town" to a meeting at the Baptist Associational office. But first he needed to go by and check on an elderly member of the congregation. To do this he bypassed off the highway onto Joe Gray road. Country people can understand what I'm saying here . . . There is nothing worse than a red clay road after a rain in the winter months. As Bro. Hodges slid along the road in his old Buick, he came upon a problem in the road.

One of the local farmers was in the road vainly trying to round up three horses that had broken through the fence. The horses were definitely winning. If you've ever tried to re-fence animals after they escape from confinement, you can probably picture the futility and frustration of this farmer.

Bro. Hodges stopped his vehicle. I'm not sure what he thought- but I know what I'd had thought- There is no way *I'm going to get all muddy in my suit.* But that's just what he did. He got out and helped get the horses in.

After the chore was done, the suit was no longer white. In fact it, and the shoes, were caked with red mud and ruined . . . Never to be worn again.

Bro. Hodges didn't tell this story to anyone. He didn't have to. The farmer, who was not a church-going man, told it. And everyone who heard it in Dry Creek told it to someone else. The story of the Baptist preacher helping to round up the horses was known by everyone in a few days.

And I'll believe it was his best sermon as pastor of Dry Creek Baptist Church. It was a sermon preached in love and with willing hands and feet. And as I write this, it's the only specific sermon I remember being preached by Kenneth Hodges. But it is a sermon that will live on in my heart and mind forever.

Not too long after this story, Kenneth Hodges was injured in a fall during a work day at Dry Creek Camp. He died about one month later. Because he was such a special friend to the camp, the Hodges Dorm was built and named in his honor and memory.

"Greater love hath no man than he layeth down his life for his friends." John 15:13

Chapter Eight

Be Still and Know...

On a beautiful Spring Saturday, my three sons and I went to work on the nature trail at the camp. As we hiked through the woods with our saw, pruning shears, and other gear, we were filled with the camaraderie of boys and their dads in the woods.

My youngest son, Terry, who was four, waded through every mud hole in the swamp. In addition, he kept up a steady stream of four years' old questions such as, "Daddy why does that water move in the creek?"

In addition to working on the trail, we brought Ziploc bags to pick huckleberries. In late May the huckleberry bushes near the creek are always full of ripe juicy berries.

The huckleberry is a wild type of blueberry. It is half the size of a tame blueberry. It takes a great deal of picking to get a decent amount of berries . . . But the picking is definitely worth the trouble. As we picked berries, the thought of hot huckleberry cobbler topped with ice cream gave me all the motivation I needed.

I gave my two older sons instructions: Look carefully in the bushes for snakes before picking. My second instruction was this: You must pick twenty berries for every one you eat. They laughed when I quoted rule number two. As I watched the purple stains grow around the edges of their mouths, I'm not sure my ratio was being followed.

...But four year old Terry was a different story. After twenty minutes he had picked about ten berries and asked somewhere in the neighborhood of three hundred questions. After answering many questions, which always led to another question, I found myself rapidly losing patience.

Finally I encouraged him to go sit on the creekbank and

watch Bundick Creek flow. I reminded him that downstream from here is where we swam during the summer. He found a seat on the bank and I returned to a time of peaceful berry picking.

As I picked, I kept an eye on Terry. I couldn't help but notice he was talking. I thought he was probably playing with one of his imaginary friends. (Just a few minutes earlier, he'd told me "He was Roy Rogers and this horse was named Trigger.")

After a few minutes of this self-absorbed talking, he called over to me.

"Daddy, I've been talking to God."

I replied that I was glad. Then I inquired, "Well, what did He tell you?"

"Daddy, I was thanking him for picking huckleberries and swimming in the creek and lots of other things."

We then conversed about how being out in nature makes us want to talk to God. Terry showed a great deal of insight when he told me, "Daddy, when you're outside like this, you just think about God don't you?" I felt a lump in my throat and it wasn't because of the huckleberry I'd just eaten.

As Terry returned to roaming about and I went back to berry picking, I was reminded of a scripture. I couldn't quote it in the woods, but when I got home I looked it up. It was Matthew 21:16 where Jesus said, "Out of the mouths of babes . . . thou has perfected praise."

We can surely learn a great deal from children. Their faith is so pure and innocent and many times their insight is keener than ours. My son had reminded me of something I knew so well: When we get out in God's world and become surrounded by nature, we will feel close to God . . . and want to talk with Him.

As I thought about this, I recalled one of my favorite scripture verses:

Be still and know that I am God.   Psalms 46:10

Because most of us live in a fast-paced society, we don't get out where it is really quiet. We move daily in a lifestyle that is never at rest or silent. Because of this, we can never claim this verse as the ***promise*** it is. *If we get still . . . we will feel God's presence.*

As the three boys and I hiked out of the swamp, I realized how important time together like this was. The investment of time I make in my children pays rich dividends. In addition, making sure they are out in the marvelous beauty of God's world is another responsibility I have.

As we walked I silently thanked God for all of the rich blessings He'd given me. As I watched my boys walking together along the trail, I thanked God for the blessing of my family. I also thanked Him for the beauty of nature and how it teaches me so much about His majesty. And then I thanked Him for all of the many, many everyday things that make life so special . . . things like picking huckleberries on a warm day in May.

Chapter Nine

Reas Weeks

I never knew Reas Weeks . . . but I sure know some good stories about him. Reas, (pronounced "Reese") was a bachelor in Dry Creek who lived on the bank of Bundick Creek. He lived way back in the woods, never owned a vehicle and supported himself by fishing, hunting, and gardening.

Mr. Frank Miller always told the story of once when Reas and another man became lost in Bundick swamp hunting. They spent the night in the woods- cold, hungry, and miserable. The next morning at daylight they finally stumbled up on Reas' shack. But Reas was confused, and still addled from being lost in the woods all night. It seemed they had approached the cabin from the opposite side he thought they were on. He exclaimed, "I know that's my cabin, but the chimneys on the wrong end."

But my favorite Reas Weeks story involves what he was best at- fishing. He was known as the best creek fisherman in our area. My dad tells the story from his childhood of the school bus picking Reas up along the road. When Reas boarded the bus he laid a 40-pound catfish on the bench by my dad. Reas was going to the community store to sell this fish.

Another of the Miller brothers, Mr. Jay Miller, was a neighbor to Reas Weeks. He related as to how he was always amazed at the large catfish Reas hooked in Bundick Creek. Mr. Jay, an excellent fisherman himself, marveled at why Reas could snag the big ones but he never did.

He told me he finally asked Reas, "Why can you catch the big ones but I can't? We set lines in the same holes and use the same bait." Reas Weeks smiled and said, "Jay come with me to the barn." At the barn Reas got out a large bucket that had his hooks and lines carefully wrapped around it. He took a whet rock out of his overalls and began sharpening a hook. Then he stated, "Jay, if you're gonna catch the big ones, you've got to keep your hooks sharp. Those big catfish have tough mouths. A dull hook won't set but a sharp one will."

I smile as I think of this story. Then I always recall the spiritual message of this story. Jesus has called us to be "fishers of men." If we are going to effectively reach others for Him, our hook had better be sharp. In my life I've found that this is only done by spending time with Jesus. As we study His word, the Bible, and fellowship with God in prayer, our lives will always be sharpened for His use.

Yes, I never knew Reas Weeks . . . He lived before my time in Dry Creek. But all of my life he'll remind me to keep my "hooks sharp."

Chapter Ten

Doten

One of life's great privileges is to live near your grandparents. I am so thankful for having known all four of my grandparents very well. Additionally I am thankful for the years I also spent with my great grandparents.

My great grandmother, Theodosia Wagnon Iles, lived until I was seven. But those seven years left a deep impression on me. Even now I think about her quite often when I see a lizard at the old house, listen to a whip poor will in the spring, hear a fiddle song, or walk to the washing spot on Crooked Bayou.

We called her "Doten". Her dad built the Old House on land he homesteaded. Doten's grandfather had died in the Civil War. She lived through and experienced so many changes in her life. As a girl, an Indian gave her a fiddle... then as an older adult she saw man launched into space. What changes she saw and what a life she lived!

Doten taught me many things as I visited with her at the Old House. She had a great love of nature and the outdoors that we both shared. However the greatest lesson she taught was one she never knew she taught me...

Doten had several great fears in life. One was that any of her loved ones were going to get too cold and become sick. I recall even on hot summer days her insistence that I get "a sweater on before I catch cold." She passed this trait on directly to my dad who is still making sure his grandchildren don't get too cold.

It was only as an adult that I understood Doten's concerns about children getting sick. As I walked in Dry Creek Cemetery among the graves of those of Doten's generation, nearly every adult grave was surrounded by little graves of children who'd died young. Then I better understood why she was like that about children and sickness.

Another fear she had was of bad weather. My dad and his siblings tell of all being gathered in an inner bedroom during a coming storm. Doten would pile the children on a bed and huddle up with them awaiting the certain approaching death. My Uncle Bill says it is a miracle that any of them can now stand bad weather.

But her greatest fear was the one that prompts this writing... and the way in which her words have stayed with me for all of these years. Doten had a life long fear of death. She never told me this, but all of my older relatives spoke of it. They said she lived with a great dread of dying for all of her eighty plus years.

In the early 1960's, Doten became ill with colon cancer. She was sick for a long time. There is a picture I've seen of her in the sick bed obviously very ill. Sitting beside her is her husband, my great grandfather Frank Iles. "Pa", as we called him, looks so tired and old. It is one of the most touching and sad pictures I've ever seen.

Prior to her death, Doten was placed in Beauregard Baptist Hospital in DeRidder.

On the day she died she made two statements that have shaped my view of death. My family said she stated as death approached, "All of my life I've dreaded this moment. And now that it's here, it's not that bad at all." Later she tried to rise up in the bed, lifted her arms and said "I see Jesus and I can nearly touch him." Soon afterwards she died.

These two stories stuck in my seven year old mind. Thirty three years later, they are still there in my mind... and in my heart. Doten lived her life in fear of something we all must face... and something we need not fear when we are prepared. Then when that time came, she did not face it alone but with Jesus. Others will surmise that she had

31

a hallucination, but I simply believe she realized she was stepping over into another life.

Yes, my great grandmother taught me many lessons. But the most important and lasting lesson she taught me was about facing death... and the surety of life after death.

Jesus said,

"I am the resurrection and the life. He who believes in me will live, even though he dies; and whoever lives and believes in me will never die."

John 11:25 26

Chapter Eleven

King Mockingbird

Each day he sits up there on the highest limb on the tallest oak on the camp grounds. I call him "King Mockingbird." The area around the Tabernacle and First Aid building belong to him. He is the biggest and loudest Mockingbird around. It is easy to recognize him high up in the oak tree. His beautiful loud singing soars above all the other noises of camp life.

Other mockingbirds dare not fly into his tree knowing a good pecking awaits any intruder. Resident cats and camp dogs steer clear of his territory knowing from past experience how fierce he is. Even as I walk under his tree I go with all due respect knowing the inviting target a bald headed camp manager makes for a territory loving mockingbird.

And can he sing! There's nothing prettier than the song of a mockingbird on a clear morning. As I hear him cheerfully sing, I'm reminded that things may be bad in many parts of the world, but in his area, all is in order.

As I think of King Mockingbird, I'm reminded of the great God who oversees Dry Creek Baptist Camp. He has blessed this ministry beyond any words that we have to describe.

In addition to creating the beautiful song of this bird, He is continually working in the lives of people who visit this place called Dry Creek. When you visit Dry Creek, be sure to stop and listen to King Mockingbird. And be sure to remember, and worship, our great God who created him.

Curt Iles

Chapter Twelve

Mrs. Helen

Every season at Dry Creek is beautiful in its own way. The winter months are no exception. Winter group camp fires are my favorite event at the prayer garden. My favorite camp fire story is about a lady called Mrs. Helen.

Mrs. Helen came with a Sulphur Ladies group several winters ago. I immediately liked her. Her bright eyes and great attitude did not show her 83 years of age. As their group went to the Prayer Garden late Friday night she stated that she could not make the walk down the trail in the dark. I quickly volunteered to transport her in my truck through the backwoods road.

These ladies had a wonderful time at the Prayer Garden! As they sang to the accompaniment of a guitar the music echoed throughout the pines. The fire crackled as testimonies brought forth both laughter and tears. For nearly two hours these ladies had wonderful fellowship out in the beauty of God's handiwork.

As the fire died out, the ladies reluctantly headed back up the hill towards the Adult Center. As Mrs. Helen and I drove back through the woods she excitedly shared about what a wonderful time they'd had. It was at that moment when I drove off in a mud hole and the truck became stuck. Try as I might to get out, I only succeeded in getting really stuck.

So here we were...ten thirty at night...stuck in Bundick Creek swamp. Finally I told Mrs. Helen, "I'm sorry to have to leave you, but I've got to go get help and the tractor." My new friend sweetly replied, "Sonny, don't worry about me... I won't be alone. God is right here with me."

Well, I returned as quickly as I could. There was Mrs.

34

Helen sitting peacefully in the truck. She said, "The Lord and I just had a wonderful time of fellowship." We pulled the truck out and were on our way. When we finally drove up to the Adult Center, it had been over thirty minutes since the other ladies had returned.

All 39 of them were standing outside in concern for the whereabouts of their oldest member. As I sheepishly began to explain to the leader of our predicament, Mrs. Helen, this sweet 83 year old saint, blurted out,

"Oh don't worry about us we were just parking in the woods."

I could feel my face (and bald head) turn red as they all roared with laughter!

As they say "All's well that ends well." I'll never forget my encounter with a special lady called Mrs. Helen.

Chapter Thirteen

Most Likely to Succeed

It was Saturday in the middle of the busy summer camp season. After a great week of youth camp I was enjoying lunch with some of our summer staff. Across the dining hall a group was having their 10 year class reunion. I enjoyed watching them as they laughed and visited after being apart for ten years.

All of these guests were former students from my years as a high school teacher and administrator. As I observed them my mind drifted back to so many warm memories of seeing them grow up.

A group of these former students came over to me with an old tattered red yearbook. They giggled as they showed me a picture from twenty five years ago. There I was sitting on a stack of encyclopedias in my early 1970's bellbottoms. Under the picture of me and one of my lifelong friends was the caption:

Senior Boy and Girl voted Most Likely to Succeed

The staffers sitting around me really enjoyed the picture. Especially my long hair!

I'm still amazed at pictures from that time period when I realize how long we wore our hair then. It was hard for this group of staffers to believe their bald middle aged director once had long hair and bangs!

Well, the former students left, laughing, hunting someone else to embarrass. All of the summer staff returned to eating what was probably our twentieth hamburger lunch of the summer.

Then I couldn't help it.... I turned to these staffers and said, "Well, can you believe someone selected "Most likely to succeed" by his classmates would end up being just an old camp manager?" Their reply was immediate and impassioned. It was best stated by Wendy, our recreation director who has worked at Dry Creek for four years: "Bro. Curt, what could be more successful than being involved in seeing lives changed daily by the Lord?" One by one they chimed in on the opportunities we have at camp to be a direct part of what God is doing.

I smiled at their reply... Because I felt the same way. More than anything to me, success is to be a part of where God is working... and I've never seen a place where He works more consistently than camps. I recalled the past week when over forty young people accepted Jesus as their personal Savior and many others made life changing commitments.

I thought about Wendy. How I've watched God work in her life through camp over a period of years. As a result of this experience she is in seminary seeking God's will on a vocation in the camping ministry.

Then I thought back to an event in my life that happened about the time of my bell bottomed long haired picture. I was at summer camp youth camp at Dry Creek the same camp where I now serve as director. God really spoke to my life and heart concerning giving my vocational choice to His will. During the invitation time, in a moment that is still clear in my mind, I went to the front of the Tabernacle and simply told God, "I'm ready to do whatever You want me to do. Just lead and I'll follow." Little did I know that decision would eventually lead me back to manage the very camp I grew up in.

If you measure success by large bank accounts, titles before and after names, or worldly fame, I'm not much of a success. But if true success is measured in feeling you are making a positive difference... and having a small part in seeing God work miracles in people's lives... and watching the Wendys of this world grow into Christian leaders, then I guess you could say I am very successful.

I'm so thankful God has given me the privilege of being part of the camping ministry. What a joy to be on the cutting edge of what He is doing! Each day I get to serve Him. Yes, most of the time it is not glorious and sometimes frustrating but I'm in a place where I know He is working and I have the awesome opportunity to be a part of it all.

Chapter Fourteen

Jesus was a walker. . .

You ask me why I'm a walker
Up and down these country roads
It's not real easy to explain
So I'll give an example to you.
You see, Jesus was a walker.
That's the only way He knew to go.
He walked on dusty roads and traveled in the hills.
He hiked through the mountains,
Where the view is nice and real.
Jesus knew a secret
That I'll now share with you:
When you're out walking in nature,
You can feel God speaking to you.
As you walk where it's quiet and peaceful,
The world's troubles will soon disappear
And you will feel God's peace
As He draws you near.
Yes, Jesus was a walker.
He even walked out on the sea.
And as I walk through these woods
I feel Him walking with me. . .

Chapter Fifteen

Love is still love... in any language

Now where do I start in describing a passionate love affair I became involved in a few years ago. You see I didn't plan for it to be exactly like this....

I didn't plan to fall in love, and have my heart stolen, by a group of thirteen South Korean young people. So let me start at the beginning as to how my life was so touched by this special group.

When a Korean American named James Kim first called concerning a camp for Koreans wanting to learn English I was somewhat skeptical. We often hear from groups with grand ideas and many times these ideas never "take on flesh" and actually happen. And the idea of a group coming from Korea to the great metropolis of Dry Creek was pretty grand (and far fetched). But as the fall of 1996 rolled on, the ZOE (This means "real life") English Camp began to take shape and become a reality. So on the night after Christmas 1996 I sat waiting anxiously for this group to arrive from Baton Rouge via Seoul and Detroit, Michigan. Another reason for my anxiety was the fear of never removing the strong smell of Korean food cooking in our kitchen as a group of their ladies cooked a welcoming meal. The strong odors of garlic, cooked seaweed, and "Kim Chi", a fermented cabbage dish, greeted anyone entering. I thought to myself, "What have we got ourselves into for the next three weeks?"

...Then they walked through the Dining Hall door. All much younger than I had imagined (ages 9 14). All looking tired and as if they were 12,000 miles from home. Few spoke any English save giving their names and a heavily accented "Hello". They were all so quiet. Little did I know that this quietness and shyness would soon disappear!

The first couple of days were spent getting situated and recovering from jet lag. On their third day at camp we began touring Dry Creek. When we visited Harper and Morgan's rodeo pens their main interest was with the fire ant mounds. They gathered around a mound and cautiously poked it with a stick. As the fire ants came roaring out the kids emitted a loud "Ahhh" (their favorite reaction to any event or startling statement.) I explained through "Tec", one of their interpreters, about fire ants. I mentioned how newborn calves can be stung to death if laying in a fire ant bed. This brought great comment in Korean among the group. James Kim later told me that many wrote their parents stating, "In America, there are ants that will kill you."

As we rode out into the field in their van, we were followed by the rodeo bulls. Ahead of us the cowboys in their truck led us out to the resident buffalo. You should have seen and heard the commotion from these city slickers from a city of 10 million people as they saw their first buffalo up close. One commented from the van (this was interpreted to me): "I feel like we are at Jurassic Park."

Later we visited King's dairy farm. Our guests got to feed calves with a bottle. But the main event was watching the milking of the cows. Mike King explained about the process as he attached the milkers to each cow's bag. As the milk gushed through the pipes to the accompanying sound of the milk machine, many comments went excitedly back and forth among our guests. My favorite one (interpreted to me) was, "I'll never drink milk again as long as I live."

From that Saturday on, they were no longer strangers but quickly becoming friends. Their shyness was quickly disappearing also. One of the oldest boys, Won Jun, whom we called Mark, asserted himself as the resident prankster and wit. (All of them went by English names they selected during their stay at Dry Creek.) Another young boy, whom

41

I called him "Bull", quickly fit in at camp by getting a fine black eye from a swinging golf club. I watched his shiner closely hoping it disappeared before his mother saw it at the end of January. I am happy to report that Bull left Dry Creek minus his black eye.

All of their personalities continued to bloom. But of the ten boys and three girls, "Sarah" became all of our favorite. Sarah was a small frail eleven year old. She was by far the smallest of the group. She had a skin disorder that made her very shy and aloof from the other children. In addition she ate so little that I feared for her health. But she also possessed a deep curiosity of everything and everyone around her. This curiosity and her winning smile won us all over. Sarah became very dear to all of us.

In spite of the language barrier we all communicated fairly well. I learned that a smile is understood in any language. Sometimes if we were speaking to one of the young people with no adult to interpret they would become confused. The Koreans adopted a very quick solution when they became confused by our English questioning. They simply said "Bye" and quickly turned and ran.

They were all amazed at American culture. When I asked one boy what amazed him most about America, he replied, "Wal Mart."

Each week day the Koreans were busy with classes in English grammar and conversation at the White House. At 1:00 they were scheduled for lunch but never arrived on time. We jokingly called it "Korean time." I began telling them the time of an event thirty minutes earlier than it was. In spite of this they still arrived late.

So sometimes after 1:00 they would come streaming into the dining hall, books under their arms laughing and talking. It hit me that they were really no different from American school kids.

Mealtimes were special with our friends. Their diet had been one of our major concerns, but they loved American food. You should have seen them wolfing down those corn dogs. They really enjoyed any dish with rice especially Mrs. Betty's gumbo. One day Shelia Marquez cooked a wonderful Mexican lunch. They quickly showed us that their healthy appetites crossed all ethnic lines.

My favorite meal time event was when they would sing their blessing. They sang it to the tune of the song "Adiel Weiss" from The Sound of Music. After a verse in Korean they sang in English:

Thank you Lord for your love
And the blessings of this day
Thank you Lord for this meal
And I love you forever
esus I praise your name
with my heart, all my will, and all my soul.
Thank you Lord for your love.
Lord, I love you forever.

After lunch was our favorite time of the day Activity time. Our camp staff prepared an activity or field trip for each afternoon. We had some fun! You've never enjoyed yourself until you show slides about Louisiana snakes to a group of Korean youngsters who speak little English! We did every type of activity imaginable visiting a herd of wild elks, seeing emus, going to area farms, playing crazy games, shooting archery, and climbing the forestry fire tower. When our volunteer firemen brought the fire trucks to the camp for a demonstration, they were most amazed not at the red engine, but our two fire women, Doris and Kathy, dressed out in their gear. For the rest of their stay they called Kathy "Firewoman." In Korea women are not allowed to be part of the fire department.

Another enjoyable trip was to Foreman's store across the street from the camp. When they entered the room where the Cajun boudin is made, they all held their noses the entire time. This amused me after I had earlier smelled their rotten cabbage dish! Another interesting trip was to East Beauregard School where the Koreans were a big hit and especially "enjoyed" touring the school's processing center/ slaughterhouse.

Probably their favorite activity was shooting black powder rifles with Roger and Frank. They talked about it for days. In their eyes, Roger and Frank became even taller than they are (and that's pretty tall) due to this event. They had seen enough American television that they looked at Roger as John Wayne and Frank as Matt Dillon.

On the weekends they would travel to either Baton Rouge or Leesville where they would stay in the homes of Korean Baptists in these communities. After their first weekend away Yeongsu Baek, one of their leaders, announced exciting news. He shared that each of the thirteen had accepted Jesus as their personal Savior and been baptized that weekend at the Leesville Korean Baptist Church.

This was exciting news! But I honestly was a bit skeptical concerning as to if each one had fully understood God's plan of salvation. But as I observed and talked to them it became very evident that a wonderful event had occurred in their lives They had come to know the wonderful love of Jesus in their hearts!

After so much fun, learning, and building friendship our days began to draw to a close. Our entire staff became filled with sadness as we anticipated our friends leaving on Saturday. At Dry Creek we are used to groups leaving and we always miss them. But this case was so different Our Korean friends had been with us for 24 days and we knew that we would probably never see them again on this earth.

During their last week with us is when the famous ice storm of 1997 hit Southwest Louisiana. At Dry Creek we mainly received sleet and fortunately did not lose our electricity. The Korean youngsters were amused at our excited reaction to white stuff on the ground because South Korea is much colder than Louisiana.

On Thursday they entertained over one hundred of our community lunch guests. No longer were they the shy children who'd arrived after Christmas. Each stepped to the microphone and spoke in surprisingly good English. "My name is Paul. How are you doing? I like soccer. Have a good day!" Everyone had a great time at this meal. After the meal they all received Dry Creek T shirts that we each autographed. That evening all of them went to Mamma Lee's restaurant for the Oriental buffet. They had a time!

Friday was a cold day as all of our weather had recently been. Being this was the Koreans last full day here, many visitors arrived from Baton Rouge and Leesville. On Friday night they held a party at the Lodge. Everyone shared through tears of the friendship and love that had grown. Then we went to the prayer garden for a camp fire. Everyone gathered closely around the fire to stay warm but there was already a special warmth on each person's face as we sang and laughed together.

To the accompaniment of a guitar they performed a Korean folk song replete with a folk dance. As the Koreans danced around the camp fire I felt as if I was in a faraway country instead of Dry Creek. (I just hoped no Baptist preacher walked up at that time to see folk dancing around the camp fire.) After more singing they brought out gifts for all of our staff. They had put much thought and love into the presents they gave us. Angela Marquez then introduced them to another American treat S'mores around the campfire.

Many a marshmallow went to a fiery death during this time.

Well, Saturday finally arrived and time came to leave. I've never liked good byes and this was one time I especially dreaded. When they came to the office everyone cried, including all of our staff. We all hugged and went outside where we joined hands and prayed together. Then they loaded up and were gone.

Later as I walked to the lodge it seemed so bare and empty. Stopping under the pines I thanked God for the privilege we have of serving so many people. And I thanked Him for this special opportunity of Dry Creek Baptist Camp being part of His mission. In this case we didn't have to go to a foreign country... They came to us. And they came from homes where Jesus Christ was not known. They left here with God's love in their hearts.

As I continued walking under the pines I caught a sense of an event far off in the future... Seventy years later in fact. An elderly Korean woman in her eighties named Soo Jung is surrounded by her great grandchildren. For the hundredth time her grandchildren ask, "Tell us again about your trip to America as a little girl" And Soo Jung smiles as she looks at her surrounding three generations of family knowing they've been reared to know the Jesus Christ she met years ago in America. And she begins again to tell her story, "Well, I was very young but I remember it as if was yesterday. America is a beautiful country and I saw so much. But what I remember best are the people."

And she dreamily smiles as she recalls the faces of long ago in a special place called Dry Creek. And one of her grandchildren asks her, "What was your American name?"

Soo Jung replies, "They called me Sarah." And once again she recalls the warm love she felt there and remembers that love is still love... in any language.

Curt Iles

Book Two:
Stories from the Back Pew

Introduction

I grew up in a wonderful church. What a joy to be part of something for all of your life. So much of my training and encouragement came from the good folks of Dry Creek Baptist Church. These stories come from my heart about a church that I love greatly because it is a church that unconditionally loved me as I struggled and grew up in it.

Chapter Sixteen

Funny Things Happen in Church

It seems that many times the most hilarious moments occur during the most serious and solemn events. Many of the funniest things I've ever seen have happened in church. I guess it is because a great part of my life has been spent in the pews. .. and I have this really bad habit of watching people. I've seen killer horseflies attack preachers, singers forget their words, dogs enter the church to worship, and drunk people come to the house of the Lord. Many times I've seen children do, and say, the darnedest things... and I've seen their parents react in very memorable ways. But my favorite church story is this one...

Every Baptist preacher worth his salt knows how to bring a sermon to a dramatic end as the time comes for the invitation. It is now time for the altar call for those whom God is speaking to. "Now I know the Lord is speaking to someone here. If He is, now is the time to move."

Those were the words of our pastor in the early 1970's, Kenneth Hodges. During the Sunday night service in the spring of that year, Bro. Hodges spoke the exact words quoted above. But the reply he got came from an unexpected source.

On the front row sat Bro. Hodges wife, Virginia. Beside her sat their daughter Pam, who was about five years old. Down the pew was Ruth Young Taylor and her daughter Marla, also age five. As the two ladies and their daughters stood for the invitation, and the hymn "Just as I am" was called out for the closing song, a voice was heard from the front pew. This voice said,

"Hi, my name is Dottie. Can I come over and play?"

It was one of the girl's doll and "it" had come alive and

51

was talking. As Dottie continued to talk, Bro. Hodges got really red in the face. He stated, "When the Lord is speaking, Satan will always try to distract you." Well, he was right. Everyone was plenty distracted as Dottie continued to speak. We teenagers were beside ourselves on the back pews. (Two rules to remember: teens should never sit in the back of church and children with talking dolls shouldn't sit on the front pew.) I remember my sister Colleen shaking she was laughing so hard. Mrs. Hodges and Ruth Taylor were practically tearing the doll apart trying to find the button or string that activated Dottie's "vocal cords."

All this time, Dottie continued to tell us her likes, dislikes, and philosophies of life. "Do you like tea?" "Let's be friends." " I've always liked Mondays."

Finally one of the mothers accidentally moved the arm that made Dottie talk... and she hushed as quickly as she had begun.... But the invitation time was a shambles. Bro. Hodges was mad at his wife and daughter. The ladies were embarrassed... and we teenagers were still fit to be tied.

Dottie never appeared again in Dry Creek Baptist Church (My dad said she moved her letter to a "sister church of like faith."). And never again did these two ladies and their daughters sit on the front pew.

Chapter Seventeen

When the K.K.K. Visited Dry Creek Church

This is a story pieced together as told me by my great grandfather, Frank Iles, and Uncle Rob Lindsey. As a boy in church, I listened as "Uncle Rob" would tell this story each year at homecoming. In my mind I could see the torchlight and the robed klansmen walk into the church...

The late 1920, when our church was newly organized, was a time of great change in our community and nation. The pain of reconstruction still lingered in our part of Louisiana. Men who'd fought sixty years ago in the Civil War still lived in Dry Creek. These old veterans rubbed shoulders with men who'd grown up never venturing past DeRidder yet had been to France and Belgium during World War I ten years before.

All of this great change had brought about much upheaval and prejudice. This unrest, fueled by the new communist movement in Europe, had helped resurrect the Ku Klux Klan throughout the South.

It was with this backdrop that Dry Creek Baptist Church held a revival. This was before a church building had been constructed. A brush arbor was built for worship and the revival began. From all accounts, God moved in a mighty way. Many lives were changed and the true foundation for our church was laid.

It was during one of the revival services that this story occurred. Many folks had arrived for the service in their wagons, on foot, and a few cars. As the singing began and dusk fell, two local boys hid in the nearby trees plotting evil. As the service continued these boys began hollering and making animal noises, throwing rocks, and generally trying to disrupt the service.

53

The lanterns and torches were lit and the singing continued in spite of the boys persistent aggravations. It was at this point that a group of about ten men riding horses approached the brush arbor. As they were illuminated by the torchlight, it was evident they were robed and hooded Ku Klux Klansmen.

The singing stopped as two of the men dismounted and approached closer. My great grandfather said the only sound was of the boys in the nearby woods tearing through the underbrush escaping the wrath of the K.K.K.

As all present held their collective breath, the two klansmen walked down the center aisle to the front. The spokesman turned and addressed the congregation, "We've all heard about what is happening here. We approve of what is going on here. We want to remind everyone we are watching how people are behaving in this community."

With no further word the two men walked out, got on their horses and the group of Ku Klux Klanners left. For a long time no one spoke a word. Then the service resumed after the K.K.K. visited Dry Creek Baptist Church.

Chapter Eighteen

Baptizing in Bundick Creek

When I cross over Morrow Bridge I always look down at the creek. The creek just south of the bridge is one of my favorite spots. It is where I learned to swim and the site of many a wonderful summer afternoon spent swimming and playing. But this spot on Bundick Creek was also the site of church baptisms when I was a child.

Before we had our present church, the old church that sat on the campgrounds had no baptistery. So everyone who was saved was baptized in either the camp pool or the creek. If a person met the Lord during winter, they either waited to warm weather or went to the neighboring church at Sugartown where they had a baptistery.

When baptisms occurred at the creek, we would all drive down Morrow Bridge road to Bundick's Creek after the morning service. There our church would gather on the bank while others stood on the bridge. The children would all be warned not to throw rocks in the water from the bridge during baptizing.

As those taking part in the ceremony would begin to wade out, we would always sing "Shall We Gather at the River." I can still hear the sounds of that song echoing off the surrounding woods.

Then our pastor would wade out into the water about waist deep. Every person participating would be in their normal clothes. No waders for the pastor or gowns for the new members. I still recall the gasps and chattering teeth as folks waded out into the cold creek water. If you've ever swum in Bundick's, you know it is cold even during the summer. I've always thought you had to be really serious about following Jesus to wade out in that cold water in early May.

Because of the water temperature, baptisms in Bundick Creek didn't take long. Everyone would file back to their vehicle and head home. Only a cloud of dust would be left behind reminding folks that there had been baptism in the creek.

One particular time stands out in my mind. Just as the pastor was in the midst of baptizing a new convert, the ceremony was unceremoniously interrupted. Unknown to everyone prior to the start of baptism, some of our church boys had wandered around the bend up the creek. There they had discovered a whole case of empty beer cans left behind on the creek bank. Being typical country boys, they had to launch them in a flotilla into the creek. Their timing could not have been worse. Just as our pastor had his arm raised preparing to baptize the first of three converts, the beer cans floated under the bridge into the baptism location. I'll never forget the look of horror on the member's faces as Budweiser cans floated among the folks in the creek.

I don't remember all of the participants in this misdeed. I only remember seeing Mrs. Dee Farmer leading her son, Wesley, away by the collar when the service ended. This event occurred in the late 1960's. It is probably no coincidence that about this time our church began planning a new sanctuary with an indoor baptistery.

Shall we gather at the river?
Where bright angels' feet have trod
With its crystal tide forever
Flowing by the throne of God
Yes, we'll gather at the river
The beautiful, the beautiful river
Gather with the saints at the river
That flows by the throne of God.

1. "Shall We Gather at the River," by Robert Lowry, 1864- Public domain

Chapter Nineteen

The Tomb is Still Empty

As a child, the first thing I would do when we arrived at church on Easter Sunday was rush to Mrs. Mosley's primary classroom. Going into the room I would find the object of my interest. There on a table was a model of Jesus' tomb. The tomb was made out of modeling clay and decorated with twigs for trees, and Easter basket grass for landscaping.

Mrs. Lucille Mosley taught the primary Sunday school class at Dry Creek Baptist Church for all of my early years. Primaries was the old term given to 6-9 years old. Our class met in the red brick building that is now the camp office. As a boy this was part of our church facilities.

Each year several weeks before Easter, Mrs. Mosley set up her Easter display on one of the classroom tables. To my eight-year old mind it was wonderful. It was evident that Mrs. Mosley had spent much time preparing this display for our class.

In addition to the items described above, she added dirt, small figures representing the guards, and a small round stone covering the opening of the tomb. As we gathered around the display on the Sundays prior to Easter, she would tell us all about the Easter story.

I always knew that when Easter morning arrived a surprise awaited all of us. Hurriedly my sister Colleen and I would go to the classroom. As always, the stone was rolled away. Just like Mary and Peter we would peer into the tomb to see that it was empty.

Throughout my childhood years and even into my teen years, this empty Easter tomb was a Dry Creek tradition. Even as a teen, making sure no one noticed, I would quietly slip into the classroom on Easter morning, and once again look at the empty tomb.

As Mrs. Mosley aged, she reached a time when she no longer taught primaries or displayed the Easter tomb. But she and her family, husband Curtis and sons John and Carl, continued to be the most faithful members of our church. They once received an award for not missing Sunday School for over ten years.

One by one her family passed away. First her husband died. Then in a two year period in the early 1990's, both John and Carl died. She was left alone at her home on Greentown road. Her health continued to decline but her love for God and faithfulness to her church never wavered.

I was gone to Tennessee when she died. I was unable to attend her funeral, something I've always regretted. When I returned home, I went to her grave at Lindsey Cemetery. As I stood there it hit me- Really, Mrs. Mosley is not here. Only her body is buried here. Her tomb is empty also. The real Mrs. Mosley- her soul- is with Jesus.

It's been many years since my first encounter with Mrs. Mosley's Easter tomb, but I always think about it each year at Easter time. I'm so thankful for the dedication of this simple country woman who left so many impressions on my life.

And even now I run with childlike wonder on Easter morning to be reminded of the glorious truth of the gospel- *That Jesus is the Son of God and He is alive.* The tomb is still empty!

I am the resurrection and the life. He that believes in me will live, even though he dies; and whoever lives and believes in me will never die.

- The Words of Jesus in John 11:25-26 again.

Chapter Twenty

Leaning on the Everlasting Arms

"The eternal God is thy refuge, and underneath are the everlasting arms."
-Deuteronomy 33:27

I know it is still there . . . page 276 in the old Broadman hymnal . . . That old classic hymn "Leaning on the Everlasting Arms." I can hear in my heart Nell Christopher playing the opening lines as we sang:

What a fellowship what a joy divine
Leaning on the everlasting arms
What a blessedness what a peace is mine
Leaning on the everlasting arms
Leaning on Jesus . . . Leaning on Jesus
Safe and secure from all alarms
Leaning on Jesus . . . Leaning on Jesus
Leaning on the everlasting arms.

As we'd get to the chorus and the ladies would drag out "Leannnnnnnnnng." I can hear my dad's loud voice echoing out "Leaning on Jesus."

When I hear this song, I still think of Him . . . Yes, I think of Jesus and how I've leaned on Him and He has never failed me yet. I've never seen Jesus let anyone down when they lean on Him.

But I also think of a man I'll always associate this song with: Rob Lindsey. "Uncle Rob" was to me the representative of the pioneer Dry Creek that I've always been fascinated with. Born in 1887, he was 89 when he died in 1976.

...And Leaning on the Everlasting Arms was his favorite song. Anytime we had fifth Sunday singing or any

opportunity for a request, he would say, "Sing 276 - *Leaning on the Everlasting Arms.*" As a boy I would watch him as we sang his favorite. On the chorus when we'd get to the "Leaning . . . Leaning . . ." part, he would close his eyes and sing from his heart. I pictured in my mind the struggles, trials, and tribulations he had probably been through in his long life. As we sang and I watched him, I was sure I could lean on Jesus too.

But what made Uncle Rob so special to all of the boys in Dry Creek was his car. All of the years I knew him, he drove a 1931 Model A Ford. I can still see it in my mind. Shiny black with red spoked wheels. We'd wait outside on Sunday morning just to see him pull in at the old church.

He'd park it right out front and come in. He was always dressed in a white shirt with a black cowboy necktie. After church he would often let us boys sit in the car or he'd pull the hood and let us look at the engine. The hood was in two parts and opened up on the sides like a winged bird.

Uncle Rob and his car were also a source of fun for us. He never traveled more than 25 miles per hour as he putted up and down the roads of Dry Creek. This gave great occasion for me and my childhood bike-riding friend, David Cole. We would see Uncle Rob coming to the post office, then located in Ryan Harper's store. When he left, we would pedal furiously behind him and pass him up on our bicycles. You've never had fun until you pass a vehicle up on your bicycle! Not knowing how to leave well enough alone, we'd ride to the next bridge, hide underneath it in ambush and overtake him again as he passed us again. I can still hear him yelling out the window, "You boys go on home and find something better to do."

Even as I write this I'm embarrassed to how we did this. In fact I know when my parents read this, I'll probably be punished for my sins of thirty years ago. I bet Olen and Eva

Cole will take David's bicycle privileges away when they hear about our misdeeds of childhood.

In spite of our foolishness, I loved Uncle Rob Lindsey. He was a link to the old Dry Creek. A reminder of the time when Indians roamed our area and no bridges existed over Bundick or Dry Creek. Back to the time when folks attended church once monthly. During Uncle Rob's life, he saw the first airplane fly over our community and later watched on television as the first man walked on the moon. He and his car will always be symbols to me of the bridge between the old Dry Creek and the modern world we live in.

As one of the patriarchs of our community, Uncle Rob would be called to the front of the church at Homecoming and reminisce about the beginning of Dry Creek Church and community.

He would share about the beginnings of our church. I could envision brush arbors, services by coal oil lamp, and dinner on the grounds when it really was eaten outside under the trees.

In 1971, when our church moved to our present location, he quickly claimed his seat in the new auditorium. He sat on the second pew from the back on the right side. His place was on the middle aisle side where he could lean his elbow over the seat edge. This was his special place and no one took it out of respect for Uncle Rob Lindsey.

Even today when we sing that old song, I still want to look back to that pew. In my mind I still see him, eyes closed, maybe a tear in his eye as he slowly rocks back and forth singing,

> *What have I to dread what have to fear?*
> *Leaning on the everlasting arms*
> *I have blessed peace with my Lord so near*
> *Leaning on the everlasting arms*

Leaning... Leaning...
Safe and secure from all alarms
Leaning ... Leaning...
Leaning on the everlasting arms.

Chapter twenty-one

The Sermon in the Hayfield

Love is patient and kind. . .   I Corinthians 13:4

As far back as I can remember, I've been around Ed King. He has always been, and still is, one of my favorite people. As a boy in Dry Creek Church I loved to hear Ed King lead the singing. His kind nature and mellow voice were always a delight to my ears and heart. In addition to leading the singing, Ed King was a well-respected deacon. We always respectfully addressed him as "Brother Ed."

Ed King operated a dairy north of Dry Creek. He and his wife, Kat, worked hard on their farm. Mrs. King was the postmaster in our local post office. They were, and still are a couple who always showed love to others.

The compelling trait I noticed as boy about Ed King was his kind and gentle nature. When you looked at him, you always could tell how hard he had worked. When you shook his hand, it was the strong and firm handshake of a man who had labored hard. His hands were leather tough and gnarled. But when a person first met Mr. King, they did not notice the hands, but the kindness that showed in his eyes. Probably the most important thing Ed King ever did for me was a sermon he once preached to me . . .

As a teenager, the Kings would hire me to help haul hay. Mrs. King would drive their old green Dodge truck as we loaded the square bales on the bed and trailer. I recall on hot sunny day how the old baler kept breaking down time after time. Each time, Ed King would methodically repair the baler. Never did he seem bent out of shape or complain. As he worked, he carried on a normal conversation with me. As he repaired a belt or pulley, he'd tell some interesting story about one of the milk cows, or what his wife, whom he called "Kitten" was cooking for supper, or ask how school was going for me.

All this time he seemed unaffected by the continued mechanical malfunctions. On the fifth baler breakdown, I expected a temper tantrum or fit, but Mr. King went right on as if this latest setback was nothing to get excited about.

We finally finished the job just before and dark and just after the seventh breakdown. I would have gladly helped haul that baler to Three Bridges and dumped it in. However, as we loaded the last bales high up in the barn, Ed King merrily worked on.

Later as I thought about it, I realized that Ed King had taught me a very important lesson that day. It's one that I'm still attempting to learn. He "preached a sermon" in the hayfield that day. Through his actions and attitude he showed me how to handle disappointment and obstacles.

Now I'm as unmechanical as they come- all thumbs. But when the crescent wrench slips and I knock the bark off my knuckles, I hesitate before I fling the wrench toward the vicinity of the woods. In my mind I recall the example I saw that day in the hayfield.

And when I face an uphill climb in life, I remember that patience and perseverance are two positive traits that go hand in hand. And I recall the day I saw those traits on display when Ed King preached his sermon in the hayfield.

Chapter twenty-two

The Greatest Day in the History of Dry Creek Baptist Church

Lay not up treasures on earth where moth and rust doth corrupt, but rather lay up treasures in Heaven
. . .Matthew 6:19-20

Now this could start an argument . . . What is the greatest day in the history of our church? Was it the day in 1925 when our church was organized? Or how about one of the great revivals held over the years? Or what about when our new building was built in the 1970's?

I believe I remember the greatest day in our church's history. Let me share about it and you'll understand why it is so special a day . . .

It was a Sunday in 1970. As time for Sunday School approached many members of Dry Creek Baptist Church gathered on the front steps of the old church in downtown Dry Creek. Soon the object of their interest came chugging up highway 113. It was an old white school bus. When I say "old" there is no exaggeration. This old bus was bringing its first load of young people to our church.

Dry Creek Baptist Church was a much different church in the 1960's than it is today. As always it was a wonderful church with the finest people in the world. But there was a great difference- There were few youth or children. Most members were older members. There were few young couples at all. I can recall Sundays where there were only four or five youth in any service.

In fact during the 1960's, one of our state denominational leaders made the statement that "Dry Creek church was dying on the vine." Before you get mad or wonder who said that, he was probably partially right. Any church without young couples, youth, or children is headed for future distress.

During this time, in 1968, a young seminary couple came as our pastor. Bob and Marcia Evans were from South Carolina and were in their early 20's. They commuted to our church on the weekends from New Orleans Seminary.

I'm not sure who had the idea to get a church bus. Someone must have had great vision and faith to buy the bus they purchased. Monette Lindsey, a bus driver at East Beauregard, was retiring a small school bus he'd driven for years. It had six seats on each side and had definitely been around a long time.

Our church bought this bus and painted it white. It was a sight! It was slow and the engine was loud. We teens laughed that it "got 5 miles to the gallon of gas and 12 miles to a quart of oil." It was routine to stop on any extended trip and add oil. You could always tell where it had been because of the blue cloud of oily smoke it left behind.

So on this Sunday morning the old bus pulled into the church parking lot. There weren't many on it that inaugural ride. But I'll always remember the look on the faces of the men as they stood in the yard watching it come to a sputtering stop. These men had worked long and hard to get the bus ready for us. I can still see the tears of several of the ladies as they saw a dream come true.

That white church bus was faithfully used. It picked up kids (and adults) for all three services, took us to youth rallies, and on bowling trips to DeRidder. I'll always remember one Saturday night when the R.A.'s went bowling in town. After bowling we were riding the bus to Master Chef. My dad took the shortcut through Twin Lakes subdivision. As we got nearly to the railroad tracks on North Street, the white bus began sputtering and backfiring. All of the boys began hollering. In the dark, fire shot out the tailpipe on each backfire. When the bus finally quit running with one final gigantic "boom," we were right in front of a wood frame home with about thirty black folks sitting outside having a barbeque. I'll never forget the large lady on the porch who stood up and hollered at the children playing in the yard,

"You kids get away from that bus. It's liable to blow up!"

...Well, it didn't blow up. And it lived to haul folks to church again. Finally it was retired for good and replaced by another bus. After several buses, our church purchased its first van. Over the years anyone who has wanted to attend Dry Creek Baptist Church has had a ride. Countless faithful men and women have driven our church buses and vans as a special unnoticed ministry for the Lord.

Now back to my original statement- The day the old white bus drove up was probably the greatest day in the long history of our church. It was the start of a special ministry. As I look around today in our church, I see so many adults who rode those early buses and vans as children and youth. Many of these early bus riders are now faithfully bringing their own families to church. I see the many young people who now attend church, in spite of little parental support, because of loving van drivers who call them and pick them up.

Our church is the way it is today because some folks nearly thirty years ago caught a vision of reaching out to our community and saw the fields "White unto the harvest." And it all started on a Sunday when an old white church bus pulled up in the parking lot.

Chapter twenty-three

Hitting it Right Down the Line...

I nervously stood in right field as a skinny thirteen year old softball player. At the plate stood the new preacher at Pleasant Hill Baptist Church. Our greatest rival in church softball was Pleasant Hill Baptist. And here we were playing them in the most important game of the year. I was by far the youngest member of the men's softball team. Usually they hid me behind the plate as catcher but today they'd put me in right field because one of the older men was injured.

So I stood there under the lights in right field knowing I was going to be tested.

Because that new preacher from Pleasant Hill liked to hit it right down the right field line.

He was probably in his late forties but looked and played like a man much younger. He always played in khaki pants and a T shirt.

This preacher switch hit from both sides of the plate. But batting left handed was what he did best and when he batted left he invariably hit line drives right down the foul line... just where I was standing. So I pounded my glove knowing that the Pleasant Hill preacher was fixing to hit it right down the line.

...That experience was my first time to encounter Logan Skiles. He was the new preacher at Pleasant Hill. Little did I know then how special this man would be in my life and the life of our church in Dry Creek.

Over the years Bro. Skiles and Dry Creek church became friends through countless softball games, numerous revivals he led in our church, and his involvement in Dry Creek Camp.

In 1992 Bro. Skiles came to Dry Creek as our interim

pastor. We could all write an entire book on the wonderful ministry he had in our church. During the years of his pastorate he taught us so much... both by his words and by his example as he bravely battled cancer. I've always felt the sermon he preached with his life as our pastor was the greatest of the thousands of messages he'd faithfully preached.

... And preach he could! Just as in softball, he "hit it right down the line." He had a way of saying things in a way that cut right to the meat of any issue. I can still hear him saying, after making a strong thought provoking statement:

"Are you there?"

Or when he preached on tithing, his oft repeated story of the man who as he awaited being baptized realized his wallet was still in his pocket. As he removed the wallet, the preacher said, "Put it back in your pocket. We need to baptize it too." Or his additional story on giving about the man who when robbed was shot and lived but they shot him again in the wallet and he died.

He had a story or saying for every situation. When he hit it right down the line he always said it with a smile but nevertheless made his point in an unforgettable way. He was straightforward and honest without being offensive.

One of my friends, Charlie Carroll, told me of when Bro. Skiles came to Pleasant Hill as pastor. The church had a reputation for fighting within itself. During Bro. Skiles' trial sermon he told them, "If I become your pastor I don't want to hear anyone talking bad about another member. If you come up to me and bad mouth someone, we're going to get down on our knees and pray right there. I don't care if we are standing in the aisle at Piggly Wiggly." Charlie said no one tried Bro. Skiles on that one because everyone knew he meant it.

One of Bro. Skiles' greatest teaching subjects was "keeping a short account." By this he meant the importance of daily keeping our sins confessed to God. I still think often of how important this is to our Christian walk and fellowship with God and other people.

What a blessing our church had to have had Logan Skiles as our pastor. I 'm sure every member of our church has their favorite story of when that preacher "hit it right down the line!"

Chapter twenty-four

The Crow and the Peacock

I was glad when they said unto me, "Let us go into the house of the Lord."
    -Psalms 122:1

As I write this during spring 1998, we are in crisis time at Dry Creek Baptist Church.

It all started a few months ago when a new door was installed at the main entrance on the south side of our church. Now this door is nice. It is glass, very sturdy, and really looks great. This project of the new door was started because of the continued problem of folks opening the old solid door and knocking someone down outside when it swung open. The last straw was when someone swung it open and knocked Glenda Hagan's casserole pan out of her hands. She had especially prepared this favorite for Sunday dinner on the grounds.

This tragedy was mourned by all who loved Mrs. Hagan's delicious cooking. So that most dangerous of all Baptist creations was named- a committee. They studied long and hard and came up with the great idea of the glass door.

On the first Sunday after the new door was installed, everyone commented on how nice it was. The only problem seemed to be that the new glass door always looked like it had been left open because of the light coming in. Joe Watson made eight trips during Sunday School to make sure it was closed.

Now I've rambled enough and got off the subject of our current crisis. But the glass door is the subject of this trouble. It seems that there is a crow that evidently has homesteaded the church property as his local domain. One day as the crow

71

hopped up to the entrance looking for crumbs left over from cookies the girl's class dropped, he spied a rival crow staring back at him.

There was only one thing to do. He began attacking the trespassing crow. I know you are probably way ahead of me. He was attacking his own image in the new glass door. I don't know if you've ever seen a bird attack his image in a glass. It is a sight to see. They don't just hit the glass once and fly off. They do it repeatedly trying to drive off the "other bird." My dad told me once of a cardinal at his house who fought "another cardinal" in the glass day after day for weeks. He eventually ended up with a flat head from banging into the window.

Joe Watson, our church custodian, was the first to notice this fighting crow. As he would drive up to the church during the day, there the crow would be flailing always at the glass door. What bothered Joe was how the crow was scratching up the new door. What was especially disgusting was the mess the crow left behind. Day after day Joe got to clean up the clear evidence that a bird had resided there.

Joe told me about it. He said he'd thought about shooting the crow. I reminded him that if he broke the glass in that $900 door, he'd never hear the end of it . . . So the saga of the fighting crow continued as Joe's personal thorn in the flesh.

This story reminded me of a story from my childhood at our old church. Thirty years ago peacocks roamed the area around the church, camp, and post office. They were owned by Ryan Harper who ran the old store where Foreman's Grocery is now located.

There were about 15-20 of them and they roamed all over. There is nothing like the loud call of a peacock right at dark. The eerie "Keeeeeyaaaaaawwwwww" unnerved many a young boy or girl at camp and initiated the first stages of homesickness. Even today when I visit a zoo and hear the call of a peacock I'm taken back to Dry Creek as a boy where peacocks roamed and you heard them all the time.

Once when I was a teenager, my dad and I stopped by the church. Dad went in the back of the old church auditorium to put up some literature. In the back of the sanctuary were four small classrooms that occupied space behind the choir area. As daddy entered into one of the rooms, an explosion occurred. It was an explosion of breaking glass, knocking around, mixed in with some human noises of distress.

I thought for sure a burglar had jumped my dad. Being the brave teenager I was, I slowly slipped back to the classroom. I did not know what I would find. When I entered the classroom, there was my dad standing but obviously shaken. Shattered glass lay everywhere in the room. He pointed to the two windows in the room. One was open and the other was closed. The closed window no longer had any glass in it.

We went to the broken window and looked out. There on the ground lay a big male peacock. He lay there dead-killed by the collision with the window. He lay stretched out on the sandy soil- long tail feathers blowing in the wind. Mr. Peacock had evidently entered the house of the Lord through the open window. When surprised by my dad, the peacock chose to go out the closed window.

As we stood there and the blood returned to my dad's face, we both began to laugh at the absurdity of this event. Just about the time I decided to go outside and pick a few feather plumes off the peacock's tail, he sat up. Groggily he shook off the cobwebs of his encounter with the window, and pranced off in search of new territories to explore.

Well, whether it's fighting crows or plundering peacocks, I've seen some real birds at church. Now don't read anything into that last statement or you're meddling. . .

Finally, there seems to be at least a happy temporary ending to the story of the crow and the new glass door. Last Sunday when I arrived early, there were about five black garbage bags hanging down from the inside handle of the glass door. These bags achieved their purpose- the crow could no longer see his rival for the ownership of the parking lot at Dry Creek Baptist Church. Joe Watson said he didn't come up with the plan- It was Bro. Don's idea. All I know is that it seems to be working. It looks like the crow won the battle of the glass door and everyone lived happily ever after.

As I close this story, I want to comment about something the crow and peacock both say to me about our wonderful church.

The peacock reminds me of how open the old church was. There was no such thing as a door lock or window latch. The church could not be locked. It was open at all times to all people.

In our present building with all of the equipment, it is not practical or possible to have an unlocked church. However, the doors of Dry Creek Baptist Church are really open to all at all times. I believe anyone, regardless of background or need, will find acceptance and the love of Jesus here. One thing I love about our church is how folks can dress any way and be accepted. Whether a person chooses to wear a suit and tie or Wrangler jeans, they will be comfortable. You don't have to dress like a peacock to be accepted at Dry Creek.

The crow reminds me of how often we fight the worst enemy we have- ourselves. The greatest battles are the ones fought in our own hearts and minds. It is so easy to keep banging our head against the glass door of life and not learn we are only hurting ourselves.

Secondly, the crow reminds me that Satan's strategy is always to get folks within the Kingdom of God to fight among themselves. We laugh at the sight of the crow beating his head over and over against an imaginary foe. The world laughs at the sight of Christians who do the same thing with each other.

Finally, we realize that the crow will keep fighting with the glass door as long as his eyes are on himself. Isn't this so true of us as humans? Only when we take our eyes off the mirror of self and look in love at others, will we be happy and fulfilled.

As we look and plan toward a new building to worship in, I'm confident that the same Lord, who laid it on the hearts of a few folks to start a church in Dry Creek, is still powerful and in charge. Whether it's a wood frame church that peacocks and dogs wandered in and out of, or a fine brick church where even crows would like to enter, or even a nice new worship facility. . . It's not the buildings that really matter. It is our living and loving Lord Jesus and the people who come to worship Him at a place called Dry Creek.

I'm glad I live in this special place where we can learn lessons from plundering peacocks and fighting crows.

Book Three:
Post Cards from Dry Creek

A summer of camp worth remembering

Introduction: A Time for Everything

There is a time for everything,
and a season for every activity under heaven:
a time to be born and a time to die,
a time to plant and a time to uproot,
a time to kill and a time to heal,
a time to tear down and a time to build,
a time to weep and a time to laugh,
a time to mourn and a time to dance,
a time to scatter stones and a time to gather them,
a time to embrace and a time to refrain,
a time to search and a time to give up,
a time to keep and a time to throw away,
a time to tear and a time to mend,
a time to be silent and a time to speak,
a time to love and a time to hate,
a time for war and a time for peace.
...He has made everything beautiful in its time.

Ecclesiastes 3:1-8, 11a

These ancient words of Solomon express how I feel when I look back over the summer of 1999 at Dry Creek Baptist Camp. It was a summer to remember. A summer those of us who lived it will never forget.

I think it was said best by Kristi Gallien, one of our special summer staffers. At our end of the summer party she stood and simply said through tears,

"It was the best summer of my life and it was the worst summer of my life."

79

As you read my thoughts from this summer, I believe you'll understand Kristi's words. I hope you enjoy reading them half as much I've enjoyed sharing them with you.

Curt Iles
August 1999

Chapter twenty-five

Let everything that has breath praise the Lord.

It's a beautiful morning as I make my first trip of the day across the camp grounds. A cool morning in early June is as refreshing as it is unexpected at Dry Creek Camp. A breeze with just a slight feel of fall blows through the pin oaks as I approach the Tabernacle.

In spite of my busyness to get to my chores, I stop at the corner of the Tabernacle by the propane tank. Because of the cool morning, the air conditioning is off and the sliding doors are open. From the open door comes the most beautiful singing imaginable. Over four hundred voices sing in unison with perfect acapella parts. This melody just seems to waft out of the Tabernacle and I can sense it rising to heaven as a praise offering to God. I can nearly sense God stopping up in Heaven as He enjoys the praise of his people.

As always, one of my favorite times of the summer is this week Florida College Camp. And one of my favorite events for this week is the inspiring singing done by these friends. As they sing, led by camp director John Kilgore, the parts harmonize in a beautiful melody:

"Lift your voice and praise Him in song,
Sing and be happy today."

Then in middle of my meditation and worship, I hear another voice singing above me. In the tall tree beside me, high up on a dead limb at the top of a pin oak, a mockingbird sings his heart out. His song is loud as he goes through this unique bird's seven sets of songs. From my vantage point his song is just as loud as the Florida College choir.

As I smile, I think about how his song is just as

praiseworthy to God as any human voice. He sings with a passion and joy. Over and over he repeats his song. Just as the Tabernacle voices sing with a happy spirit, Mr. Mockingbird has a joyful song that he cannot contain. I know that if I come by this spot four hours later, he will still be singing.

Then Psalms 150:6 comes to mind:

"Let everything that has breath praise the Lord."

Just as my friend John Kilgore leads in the Tabernacle with a visible joy and passion, Mr. Mockingbird sits on his high perch and leads in a chorus of singing. Other nearby mockingbirds respectfully join in the song, but none dare come closer to this king of the mockingbirds. As I get still, I hear the other birds mockingbirds, cardinals, and blue jays singing in the trees. Their song is done acapella also and with unique parts that blend together in a wonderful melody.

I can nearly hear this king mockingbird saying: "These campers come here every year in June and think they own this part of Dry Creek Camp. They don't know it but this area of the grounds is my kingdom and I'm only allowing them to borrow this space at my good pleasure."

I smile at the absurd thought of a talking mockingbird. But then I think about how God probably says the same thing about all of us who walk these special grounds at Dry Creek. He says to us: "Don't forget that I own this camp. I've chosen to do a good work here. I've been doing it for seventy four years. I'm just letting you borrow some space here to be in on what I'm doing. Don't you forget that this is my area?"

All of a sudden I'm awakened back to where I'm standing. In my left ear, a mockingbird sings. In my right I hear the sound of voices lifted up to God. I bow my head and thank God that I'm standing here at this special place called Dry Creek Camp.

"So I will sing praise unto thy name forever..."   Psalms 61:8

[1] "Sing and Be Happy" Emory S. Peck Copyright 1940 Stamps-Baxter Music 1968

Chapter twenty-six

A Girl Named Candace

One of my favorite parts of summer camp is seeing many of the same campers return year after year. It is so neat to watch a young person mature from an aggravating R.A. boy who'll never take a shower into a strong, robust, and immaculately groomed teenager . . . or to see a gangly freckle-faced homesick girl later return as a wonderful and beautiful counselor.

Candace is one of those campers I've enjoyed watching. I first observed her seven summers ago. She was here in early June for Florida College Camp.

Florida College is always our first camp of the summer. Early June is also the time of year when most of our baby birds leave the nest. It is always interesting to mix four hundred campers with mockingbirds and barn swallows that are on the ground, but not quite ready to fly. Most campers, especially the girls, savagely protect these birds. Even though the campers mean well, the mother birds swoop down on the campers, trying to protect "their children" from "our children."

That is how I met Candace. She was a skinny face twelve-year-old tomboy. She wore her hair in dog ears and loved to play and be outdoors. One day she came to me clutching a baby barn swallow she had "rescued." She was followed by an entourage of other girls all worried about the cute little bird.

I tried to explain how this was a stage all baby birds must go through and touching it could keep its mother from feeding it. I suggested to the girls that they put the bird back where they found it and let nature and its mother take care of it.

There was no way Candace would agree to this. She argued about the danger of cats, rain, and four hundred pairs of tennis shoes. She left with her followers, still hugging the little bird. Later during the week, she would show me her pet. It now resided in a shoebox replete with water in a jar lid and bird seed. I didn't even bother telling her this bird was a long way from being ready to eat birdseed.

I decided it was useless to argue and gave what little helpful advice I could on raising baby birds. All through the week Candace would inform me of other nests or babies she'd found. When camp ended on Saturday, she left the bird with me. She cried as she lamented on the future of her bird.

I let the now-feathered bird go and he flew off into the trees. Just as I did this, the last bus pulled out with Florida College campers . . .

The next summer I looked for Candace when campers began arriving. There she was . . . But she had changed. No longer did she have dog ears or freckles. It was very evident that my tomboy friend was changing into a lovely young lady.

As I approached Candace I made one of the worst mistakes of my camp tenure. In front of several of her friends I said, "Well, Candace I'm glad you're back to take care of the birds again." She looked at me with the stare that only a teenager can give a stupid adult. It was as if I was a Martian speaking to Queen Elizabeth. Very curtly she replied as she walked away, "I'm not interested in birds."

My faux pas left me feeling about two inches tall. I had forgotten something I already knew: When a pre-teener becomes a teen, especially girls, they change dramatically and quickly. Quickly they go from Barbies and Tonka trucks to make-up and other grown up things. I thought about Candace and the words of Paul in I Corinthians 13:

*When I was a child, I thought like a child, I reasoned like a child. When I became a man,
I put away childish things.*

Candace had put away childish things . . . and she had put me in my place as well. She had become a teenager and baby birds were no longer part of her world. Even though she would speak to me that week, I believe she never fully forgave me for embarrassing her in front of her friends.

Through each succeeding summer, I enjoyed watching Candace mature into a beautiful young woman. This summer, 1999, was her last year to attend as a camper. As I watched her with her many longtime friends (and many boy admirers), I thought to myself, "Candace, you've come a long way since your bird-protecting days."

As I walked out of the cafeteria later that week, a young camper came up to me, "Hey mister, have you seen this bird nest?" He pointed up under the porch east of the kitchen. Sure enough they're above the light fixture was a mud-daubed nest full of four baby barn swallows. Hearing our approach the birds greedily opened their beaks awaiting food.

During the next week I watched the miracle unfold. In just a matter of days the birds went from tiny, featherless, and helpless birds to a light covering of down and wing feathers. Then several days later the biggest ones were out of the nest hopping on the ground.

I'm very sentimental and love birds so I couldn't help but put some sawhorses and flagging around their staging area. By the next day they were all four on the ground. I was so glad we didn't have any camp cats hanging around. Nervously our staff watched them. Finally on a Saturday they all began to fly.

Even now as I walk the grounds and see a cigar-shaped swallow swoop by, I wonder if it is one of this year's birds.

And once again, as I look around and think of Candace, I'm reminded, and astounded, at how soon they, birds and children, leave the nest to fly.

Chapter twenty-seven

Red touch yellow, Kill a fellow

For the fourth time I go back to my seat in the tabernacle. Four hundred and fifty G.A. girls sit in rapt attention as camp pastor Ronnie LaLande does a monologue on Namaan. He is resplendent in a robe, turban, and sandals. Bro. Ronnie has been a G.A. camp fixture for seven summers. When he becomes a Biblical character, it is as if he really is that person.

I'm now getting situated after fixing the last minor emergency. It seems a counselor had a homesick camper and Monday night is the first official night of homesick season. I'm hoping now I'll get to enjoy the service and see what God is going to do in the lives of these girls.

Just as Namaan gets to the part where he is complaining about how muddy the Jordan River is compared to his crystal clear streams back in Syria, I'm tapped on the shoulder. Turning, I see James Blankenship, our summer staff leader, motioning me outside. I try to hide my disgust as I thread my way out. I think to myself, "I bet it is something he could take care of without me."

When we get outside the Tabernacle several people are gathered and James points to the flower area by the door. There is a snake. James relates, "I was sitting here on a tree bench when I saw it."

And it's not just any snake- but a coral snake. The red, yellow, and black stripes make it easily recognizable. I repeat the saying from my childhood,

"Red touch yellow . . . kill a fellow
Red touch black . . . friend of Jack."

This snake has the red and yellow stripes touching and the distinctive black nose of the coral snake. He is about two foot long- a good size for a coral snake. As I look around for a stick to kill him, I remember that the coral snake has the strongest venom of any American snake.

By now the campers and counselors on the back row have turned to look out the windows wondering what is going on. They can't see the snake, which is below their sight line, but they know something interesting is there in the flowers.

With my new found weapon I hit the snake. The only problem is my stick is rotten. It breaks apart as I strike and the coral snake is now stunned and infuriated. He instinctively heads for cover as I frantically hunt another weapon. And here is why I'm frantic: Mr. Coral snake is burrowing furiously under the edge of the Tabernacle wall. Before I can do anything only his tail is sticking out as he disappears under the wall.

Now I'm aware that Namaan is probably on his fifth dip in the Jordan River inside the Tabernacle. I don't remember any snakes in that river from the book of II Kings, but if I don't do something quick there's going to be one in this story, accompanied by more than four hundred screaming girls.

The counselors on the back row are very interested in our rodeo. Recognition of what is out there registers on their face. When I charge in the back doors to make sure the snake hasn't come under the wall, all of them have their feet tucked under their chins up on the pew. I'll never forget the look on Davy Funderburk's face. He is sitting right under the spot where the snake is trying to get in.

To my relief there is no snake inside. The floor plate should keep him out of the Tabernacle. I hurry back outside. Someone brings me a stout stick. But the coral snake is nowhere to be found. We surmise that he has burrowed up under the Tabernacle wall.

Using my stick, I begin probing in the dirt under the wall.

I'm joined now by several other brave souls, including James who is standing cautiously back eight feet away. Finally closer to the back door, I see red, yellow, and black in the dirt. He is burrowing in the dirt trying to escape. Using my stick as a rake, I pull him out in the flowerbed. Now he is in the open and determined to elude me. To our horror he heads straight for the Tabernacle door. I'm sure he thinks if he can get under the door he'll escape the tormenting devil who is hitting him.

I'm willing to do anything to keep him outside so I instinctively use my stick to rake him away from the door. He flies about six feet across the sand and wraps around James' foot.

... Now before I tell you how this story ends, I must tell you about James. I love James like a son. He is our summer staff director. And he is a city boy. And the last thing he wants is a coral snake wrapped around his leg.

So James begins a dance that is hard to describe. All I can say is not even a boa constrictor could have stayed attached to James' leg with the moves he was making. One of the guys later said, "He sure got religion when that snake wrapped around his foot."

The snake hits the ground and I hit him good. It was all over so quickly. The dead coral snake lay there. James stood back still shaking and all of us had a fine laugh at this comedy in errors.

By now Namaan (a.k.a. Bro. Ronnie) has just been cured of his leprosy and was praising God. I could've gone in the service but I just didn't think I could sit still after this.

Chapter twenty-eight

Ritalin patrol

Here I am sitting in the office of Dr. Louis Shirley in Jennings, Louisiana. Two hours ago I was enjoying lunch at camp. Boys Opportunity Camp was only a few hours old. I was enjoying my hamburger and fries when the chilling message was relayed to me:

"A camper forgot his medication."

This statement is one to be taken seriously. Adam, our counselor in dorm seven, probably doesn't know it but his happiness over the next several days depends on what happens next.

Boys Opportunity Camp is a special summer event at Dry Creek. It is for boy's ages 12-14 that need a special "opportunity" to be in a Christian setting. Most of these boys are from non-church backgrounds. They are recommended by juvenile officers and school officials. Because many of them have special needs, they often are on various medications. We've found through past experience that it is imperative they are on their medication. A three-day camp doesn't sound like it would matter, but you can believe me- it makes all of the difference in the world.

This particular camper has forgotten his daily high dose of Ritalin. I immediately know we've got to spring into action with "Ritalin patrol." I attempt to call his mother- no phone. I call the next door neighbor who brings mom to the phone. Of course she can't bring it to the camp. She has no transportation. She gives me the address and assures me the Ritalin is there.

An hour later I drive up to the house. The mother is sweating and upset. "I can't find his medication." I sit in the truck as she goes back to search again. She returns apologetically with no bottle.

Then she remembers, "I've got a prescription!" We are back in business. But the prescription is in her purse that the neighbor keeps for protection. After a long and fruitless search at the neighbor's house we have nothing.

The easiest thing would have been to return home now. But I'm determined to succeed. To return from Ritalin patrol empty handed would be bad . . . especially when I think of this camper in a cabin without Ritalin for three days.

We then call the pharmacy and request three pills. However, the pharmacist cannot help us. Ritalin prescriptions are highly regulated due to people selling them for illicit use. I understand his answer. His only suggestion is to get a new prescription from the doctor.

I haven't come this far to fail. So the mother and I (we've become friends now) load up in my truck and go to the doctor's office. It is a busy afternoon in the office as we take our seats and wait. They don't call it a "waiting room" for nothing.

Eventually after what seems like hours, we now move to the doctor's private office. The mother and I continue to visit. It is a great opportunity to share about the Lord. She shares the tragedies and trials of her life.

After about thirty minutes, Dr. Shirley comes in. He listens to our tale of woe. He happily writes out a prescription for three Ritalin pills. We thank him profusely and leave. After a quick stop at the pharmacy and then dropping off my new friend, I'm on my home. When I return in triumph, no one even realizes I was gone. But I'm back with my prize and dorm seven will be much happier because of these three small pills.

Three days later I drive the campers from Jennings home. As my new camper friend exits the van his parting words are, "Thanks mister, I really had a great time."

And I think, "So did I."

Chapter twenty-nine

God's Timing is Always Right

I wrote this poem during a particularly discouraging time in August 1998. We had dug the footings on the new snack shack/gift shop. As we got ready to pour the slab, the costs on the concrete and electrical preparation had skyrocketed. We didn't have the money we needed to start this project. Volunteers were scheduled to come in September and I really didn't know how we'd be ready.

Then just before the day to pour the concrete, a huge rain washed in all of our footings. So on a scorching August day we began to re-dig, by hand, all of the ditches and chain walls. It was very discouraging to be redoing a bad job.

This poem, inspired by one of my special friends, Mrs. Rhedia Skiles, came to me as I dug in the red clay. Now a year later as I look at the beautiful building that was completed on time with all the money available each step of the way, I can only bow my head and say how great God is.

God's Timing is Always Right
God is very seldom early
But He's always right on time.
When the need must be met by midnight,
He'll supply at 11:59
Just as Moses stood in the water
At the edge of the Red Sea,
God waits until the very end
To supply our every need.
If you wonder why He has this habit
Of waiting till the end,
He does it to remind us

He's the one on whom we must depend.
For if we worked it out early
And provided in our own strength,
We'd think we all did it
And not realize it was from Him.
All God really wants from us
Is to trust Him everyday
And to always say, "Thank you"
As He directs us along life's pathway.
Yes, God is very seldom early,
But I've never seen Him late.
In faith we can completely trust Him
To meet our needs in His own time
. . . and His own way.

Chapter Thirty

A Bright Light

"Let your light so shine before men that they may see your good deeds and praise your Father in Heaven."

It's the time of evening I love best at camp... the sun is going down, the shadows lengthen as another day slips by. In the oaks around the tabernacle, the crickets and tree frogs prepare for their nightly duet.

Campers scurry to the Tabernacle. The excitement of a good day and the anticipation of the evening service can be felt in the air just as real as the cool breeze blowing across the grounds. Everyone is full after a fine meal of chicken strips. Teenagers dressed in their new jeans laugh around the tree benches the prime location for courting and friendship at Dry Creek Camp.

I sat in the pavilion just resting. As darkness approaches I notice several outside lights aren't turned on. Irritation comes over me as I think, "Now who forgot to turn on the lights." But my irritation is quickly replaced by sadness. . . The realization hits me that Brad won't be here to turn on the lights anymore.

Earlier this afternoon we had buried Brad Robinson at Mt. Moriah Cemetery. Brad had died two days earlier when struck by a drunk driver. As I sat in the pavilion, the events of the last three days came over me again. The shock of losing Brad so suddenly, the pain of sharing the news with his staff friends, the sorrow of seeing his parents, sisters, and grandparents in such grief. Even now my head was still pounding from the tears and emotion of the day.

Then I thought about the joys of the last three days. Spanky's simple reply when I called him of Brad's death:

"I'm happy for Brad." The strong faith of our staff as they grew closer to each other and Jesus. Ryan's praise and worship with his guitar for his dear friend. Clay's words at the funeral...."The peace that passes all understanding." James story: "Wake up." In spite of my sorrow, a deep peace filled my heart as I recalled how God is faithful in all circumstances -- even tragedy.

Only those who had lived this Monday could understand when I call it a "wonderfully terrible day." . . .

I get up from my seat and go to begin turning on the lights. I guess it will be my job this evening. I wonder who will be the new light person at Dry Creek now that Brad is gone.

As I walk I think about the first time I saw Brad at Dry Creek. He came in the spring of 1998 to try out as a staffer. I remember him getting out of his truck dressed in overalls. His application had been very impressive although he was only 15 at that time. When I saw Brad there by his truck, I thought "This guy is not 15 he looks 20 years old. There was a physical and spiritually maturity about Brad Robinson that made him stand out.

That tryout weekend, Brad won our hearts with his hard work and big smile. When the weekend was over, our adult staff members said, "You better hire him or we'll never talk to you again." . . . And so began the special love affair between Brad Robinson and Dry Creek Camp.

When last summer ended, all of the other staffers went home. But I'm not sure Brad ever really went home. Very seldom did a week go by that he wasn't at the camp. My wife, DeDe, and I laughed as to how you'd see Brad everywhere youth rallies, ball games, the camp, church events. You never knew when you went to an event if he would be there flashing that big smile I will always cherish. Brad just seemed to be everywhere especially at Dry Creek where we never grew tired of having him around.

When he wasn't there in person, he was ever present in e mail or on the phone. I'd like to know how many messages I received from "DCstaffer" and "Bloodwashed." I picked at him as to how he ever had time for school with his social life, e mail, web page, and constant going.

Word kept coming back to me last fall about the tremendous revival that had occurred in Brad's school due to his deep commitment to Jesus.

I think about my favorite day with Brad. It was this spring. As a school assignment he was to "shadow" a job he was interested in. Of course, he came to Dry Creek to follow me around. He always told me he would take my job from me some day! On this day, he traveled with my mom and me to Glenmora. We were working on chartering a bus for an upcoming senior adult trip. I was so impressed as to how he met adults and visited with my mom. We had lunch at Reggie's in Glenmora. It was a special day I will always cherish.

. . . All of these memories and emotions come to me as I flip on outside lights. As I walk by the laughing campers, my mind is a thousand miles away.

. . . Then here comes Kristi. She ambles up to me with her big smile. Now Kristi is someone I love as a daughter. She is also a second year staffer but I've known her since she was born. I've watched her grow up to become the special young woman she is. Kristi says, "Brother Curt, I'm in charge of the lights now. I need someone to help me make sure I know where they all are." I start to tell her to get with another staff member but then I catch myself. . I'm learning through this to spend time with those you love. . . And Kristi is so special to me. So I reply, "I'll show you and we'll visit while we walk." So we walk and talk as we relive the events of this deeply emotional day.

. . . As we walk, I think about the picture of Brad on my dresser at home. Brad is at our home last spring. He is dressed to kill with a huge smile on his face holding his cool sunglasses. He is on his way to pick Kristi up for the Prom. It's a wonderful picture that fully reveals the full personality of Brad Robinson.

Kristi and I laugh and talk, even through our tears, as we stroll to each light. As the last light is flipped on and Kristi walks away, I just sit for a while in the coming darkness. The camp lights illuminate various areas of the camp while other areas, away from the buildings, remained shrouded in darkness. Then I think about the light of Brad's life... About how brightly it shined at Dry Creek... and Mt. Moriah Baptist Church....around LaCamp, Louisiana . . . and at Ray's Grocery and Hicks High School...how Brad's light shined brightly and consistently. How even in death his life witnessed as a bright light no drunken driver could snuff out.

And I'm confident that no amount of time will extinguish the bright light of Brad Robinson's life. He will live on in the hearts of all of us who love him. His witness will continue to shine brightly at Dry Creek long after those of us who love him are gone.

You see when a young person sells out to Jesus, as Brad did, their witness and light burns for all eternity.

The words of Jesus sum it up best:

"You are the light of the world. A city on a hill cannot be hidden. Neither do people light a lamp and put it under a bowl. Instead they put it on its stand, and it gives light to everyone in the house. In the same way, let your light shine before men, that they may see your good deeds and praise your Father in Heaven."

-Matthew 5:14 16

This beautiful poem was written by Judi Reeves, one of our special camp friends. She penned it after one of our favorite weeks of summer camp, Life Roads Youth. During this camp, the teens go out daily to witness and minister in surrounding communities.

Chapter thirty-one

The Spirit at Life Roads

It's early morning at Dry Creek Camp
Sun shines through the trees
Grass stirs in the breeze
God's saints getting ready
The Spirit, strong and steady
It's now mid morning at Dry Creek Camp
Vans enter the grounds
Young people look around
A stillness in the air
The Spirit- nothing can compare
It's mid-afternoon at Dry Creek Camp
Groups are being decided
Friends may be divided
Excitement is building
The Spirit is willing
It's mid week now at Dry Creek Camp
Excitement abounds
Praises heard all around
Young Christians are growing
The Spirit is flowing
It's the last day now at Dry Creek Camp
Some sadness in hearts
New friends will depart
The air has calmed down
The Spirit- still around
It's time to leave now from Dry Creek Camp
The love we were shown
Our gifts we have honed
We were obedient to Him
Now the Spirit flows within

We'll think often of our time at Dry Creek Camp
We met Jesus there
We learned to care
To take the Word of our Lord
The Spirit- our shield, our sword.

Chapter thirty-two

Oh, Let My Pride Fall Down, I'm a little man

The song booms out of the sound system. Over and over, the refrain says,

> *Oh, let my pride fall down*
> *I'm a little man*

It's clean up time at the Tabernacle. An hour ago this building was full of excited teenagers. Now it is empty save our staffers who've brought their brooms, floor sweep, and a week's worth of stories. When camp ends, our staffers go out to the entrance and wave goodbye as vans, buses, and carloads of campers leave out.

After the last vehicle leaves, one of my favorite camp events takes place- Sweeping the Tabernacle. It's one of the first jobs I learned as a thirteen-year-old at Dry Creek. The sound of the pews being leaned over and broom handles clacking together as staffers pretend they are light-saber wielding Jedi knights. The laughter of comradeship as everyone comes together after a long and eventful week.

And all of these working sounds are accompanied by the sound system. We allow the staffers to play "their kind of music"- Contemporary Christian music.

At the end of the sweeping they'll gather up front and have share time. This Dry Creek tradition is a privilege to listen in on. The counselors tell their stories of victories, challenges, short nights of sleep, and the lives they've seen changed. The staffers report with the latest stories of spills in the kitchen, broken water lines, and long hours in the Snack Shack. There is always a wonderful mixture of laughter, tears, and joy as our workers share.

I sit feeling as if I'm an eavesdropper on an important intimate conversation. I'm not part of their generation and don't always know their jargon. It is a special time in a special building among a very special group. How thankful I am to share this moment with these teens.

When share time is over, it's time for our staffers to go to the dorms to begin the dreaded cleaning there. As they go out someone flips back on the sound system and once again "the Supertones" are singing,

Ohhhhh let my pride fall down,
I'm a little man.
Ohhhhh let my pride fall down,
I'm a little man.

This song, one of the favorites of our teen workers, tells of the importance of remembering we are nothing without God . . . and everything with Him in control.

My two teenage sons love this same group and play this song over and over. As I've listened to the words, I've come to realize this contemporary song is very scriptural. *We are nothing without God!*

It's something I've surely learned in my life in 1999. The first part of this year was the most difficult period of my life due to a time of personal problems. During this time I struggled, and struggled greatly. But God proved Him faithful. And in spite of my troubled time, the ministry of Dry Creek Camp went better than ever.

These months taught me something- God doesn't need me to accomplish His good work. The Camp's work will go on, with or without me. This experience reminds me of what a privilege for me to be a part of what God is doing.

This difficult time was also very freeing to me personally. Because God showed me that He can do His work without me, I'm confident I don't have to do everything or play God. Additionally, the spring of 1999 showed me what a valuable staff we have. The folks who work year round at Dry Creek-Diane, Frank, Dwayne, Janet, Monse, Debra and the many others who cook, clean, and help fill the gaps, are the keys to what is going on at camp. This time makes me even more thankful for our staff and how each person's diverse talents meet the needs here.

Because God is doing such a fine and fresh work here, people are constantly complimenting the work of the camp. It's nice to hear these positive affirmations. But always in the back of my mind I hear the words of the song:

Ohhhhhh let my pride fall down,
I'm a little man.
Ohhhhhh let my pride fall down,
I'm a little man.

[1] Lyrics from the song, "Little Man" by the Supertones. Lyrics appear courtesy of BEC Recordings, Copyright 1998. By We Own Your Songs, Inc. (SESAC)

Chapter thirty-three

Perfect love casts out fear...

At 1:30 AM my truck headlights approach the driveway. It's early morning on July the 5th. My ten year old son, Terry, and I are returning from a late night all star baseball game. The game was delayed due to a three hour rain delay. During this delay, my wife, DeDe, and her parents who are visiting with us, decide they've had enough, and leave.

After seven hours of sitting, we finally finish the game after midnight as fireworks explode in the sky over DeQuincy. My eyes are blurry as I begin the one hour drive home. Terry goes to sleep in the seat beside me and I think about how neat is to enjoy the wonderful game of baseball together. I also think of how early the first day of camp will come in just a few hours.

As I approach my driveway, reflected light catches my headlights. Five figures on bicycles are sitting in my driveway. My first thought as I see the small BMX racing bikes is "staffers!" And then the thought, "I'm gonna kill them if they're out riding those new camp bikes at 1:30 AM." I ease up to the rider closest to my mailbox. From his silhouette, it is very clear this is Luke Haynie, one of our staff counselors. I say, "Hey what are you guys doing out at this time of the night?" When they all turn to look at me, I don't know any of them. They aren't staffers or any teens I know from Dry Creek. They give me an ominous look and slowly pedal off.

I drive to the house with wondering who they are and what these guys are up to at this time of night. Terry and I go into the house. I quickly lock the garage door. Terry runs water for a bath to wash the DeQuincy mud from his body. I get a glass of milk, some cookies, and unfold the newspaper.

As I sit on the couch, the dogs bark outside. I get the eerie feeling that the night riders are still out there.

Suddenly from the hallway I hear the front door swing open. A chill goes up my spine as I expect one of the mystery riders to come down the hall with a weapon in his hand and malice on his mind. When I get the courage to go to the door, which is slightly ajar, I see nothing in the blackness outside. Quickly I slam it shut, turn the deadbolt, and latch the chain. Wearily I go back to my chair. An old bluegrass song runs through my mind

"It's only the wind; children are not at the door.

It's only the wind, wind precious wind, nothing more."

About one minute later a loud knock resounds off the front door. A muffled voice can be heard outside. Now I know for sure the night riders are at my door. I wonder if I should let them in or not. I go to the door and speak through it,

"Who's out there?"

A voice responds, *"Let me in."*

Shakily I answer, *"Who are you?"*

The reply gives me the biggest scare of the night as my father in law responds,

"It's Herbert. Open the door. You've locked me out!"

I quickly unlock the lock to find my father in law standing there in his boxer shorts. He passes by me without a word, shaking his head, and quickly goes back to bed, even as I feebly attempt to explain.

Later I realize he had tried to get in the bathroom only to be blockaded by Terry who was enjoying a soaking bath after the game. Then being the country man he is, he simply went outside on the porch. . And that's when I entered the story and locked him out.

As I returned to my milk and cookies, it was now two o'clock and R.A. camp was only a few hours away. Even with the late hour I went into our bedroom and woke DeDe up to relate the story. We both laughed until we cried as we lay there in the dark.

I left for work early the next morning long before my father in law, Herbert Terry, arose. Luckily for me, I didn't see him that day. I've heard he is now laughing about this escapade. My brother in law said his dad told him,

"I thought I was going to have to give my name, rank, and serial number to get Curt to let me back in the house."

Then he added to his son,

"If you go down there to stay, make sure you don't go out on the porch at night or you'll be stranded."

Now I love to find a spiritual meaning in all of my stories. I bet you're thinking, "He's going to have to stretch it to find one on this tale." But the next day it did come to me: I had acted out of fear from the minute I saw those bike riders in my drive. Normally I'm not scared of much, but the late hour, my tiredness, and these strangers combined to put me on the defensive and the result was to lock out my poor old father in law.

I then wondered how many times I've let fear lock others out of my life. How much love, how many friendships, and opportunities have I missed because of that dangerous emotion called fear?

God, help me to be a risk taker in my relationships. To not fear giving of myself, be let myself be vulnerable . . . to not be afraid to show my human side. Don't let me allow my fears, prejudices, and presumptions to lock others out. . . Most of all, help me open the door of my heart for You to be free to shape and mold me.

In Your name, Amen.

"Perfect love casteth out fear." I John 4:18

[1] "It's Only the Wind" by the Sullivan Family Public domain

Chapter thirty-four

Seth's Big Camp Day

There is no camp like R.A. Camp . . . For those of you without a proper Baptist education let me explain what R.A.'s are- it stands for "Royal Ambassadors," our Southern Baptist mission education organization for boys. My dad, who led R.A. Camps for years, always said it stood for "Rowdy Apes."

R.A. Camp has a flavor of its own. When you mix all boys with men as counselors and leaders, the fun begins. As young boys, my three sons refused to go to Preteen camps where "there would be girls." But they couldn't wait to get packed for R.A. Camp.

Speaking of packing, many a R.A. boy has returned home with their luggage untouched. Only their Monday clothing and swim suit was used. When I served as an R.A. camp director, I could always call many of the boys by name because they wore their summer league baseball shirts, with their name emblazoned across the back, all week long.

Do you know what an "R.A. shower" is? It's what boys tell their moms when asked the question, "Did you take a shower everyday?"

"No, mom I didn't need to, I went swimming everyday."

If we had women counselors there would be more showers, more dirty clothes, and probably a lot less fun.

These things, and many more, make R.A. Camp so unique and one of my favorite weeks of the summer. But there is one trait that sets R.A. Camp apart that is no fun at all. It's a deadly disease called homesickness.

Homesickness strikes both genders and all preteen ages. However, it seems to occur worst at R.A. Camp. I'm sure

109

psychologists would like to study the reasons why. Here are a few of my theories. First of all, when girls come to camp they bring a huge number of moms as counselors. These wonderful ladies are better at comforting the afflicted. Men aren't the most gifted at helping a sobbing youngster whose only wish in life is to see his momma.

A second theory has to do with teddy bears. A few years ago we purchased a bunch of stuffed bears. We keep them in the First Aid station. I've seen many a homesick girl instantly placated by a pink stuffed bear. Go figure it.

But a homesick boy doesn't want a bear, he doesn't want another snow cone from the snack shack (I've tried such bribery many times), and he wouldn't think of crawling up in a bunk with another camper. He only wants one thing: His momma.

So let me tell you about Seth. Seven year old Seth arrived on Monday this summer so excited about camp. His mother, Molly, told us he might be a little homesick later in the week. ...But she was wrong- He was homesick by Monday lunch. I spent the afternoon visiting with him. I soon realized that here was a man going home no matter what. I've won many times in the battle of homesickness ("Let's just wait until tomorrow morning and see how you feel.") But it was clear waiting was useless, Seth was going home . . . and soon.

Molly didn't seem too surprised when she got my telephone call. Because they only lived thirty minutes away, she soon arrived to get Seth. He was a happy camper as he hugged his mother, and quickly loaded up his gear in the truck before anyone could change their mind. As they drove off I thought, "Well, Seth, I'll probably see you next year."

As I watched the vehicle drive up with Seth looking out the window, I thought back to my first camp experience at Dry Creek. I grew up four miles from the camp. When I was nine, I first went to R.A. Camp. We stayed in cabin I-1 which is now the Paint Building.

I had a great time until Tuesday afternoon. While wrestling with my counselor, I was slung off and hit my head against a bunk. That blow didn't create amnesia. It created the opposite- *Remembrance*- remembrance of how badly I needed to see my momma. Nothing could convince me otherwise.

The next summer was better- I made it until Wednesday. It is with great pride that I share that my eleven-year-old summer I made the entire week. It is worth noting that my success had less to do with my maturity than with the fact my dad was now the camp director.

I laugh as I recall my debut at camp. Then I think about my youngest son, Terry. Terry holds two Dry Creek records that may never be broken. Both records were set the same year when he was seven. His first record is "Shortest distance from home for homesickness." Terry broke the longtime record held by my childhood friend, David Cole. Terry's new record is one mile.

Terry's second record is even more impressive. It reads, "Shortest time at camp before leaving home homesick." That year he went home during Monday lunch. I saw him in the cafeteria line, clutching his stomach, with the worst pained expression. I wondered if maybe he already had spent his five dollars at the snack shack and had a stomachache. But I quickly recognized what it was. Only those who've suffered homesickness can know how it is truly a physical illness.

I thought for a while this year Seth might break Terry's shortest duration record. But being the competitive father I am, I held Seth off until the afternoon to keep the old record intact.

As the sun begins to set behind the trees on Monday evening, I imagine Seth is happily at home watching "Home Improvements" on television. I look around warily as campers stream toward the evening service. Approaching darkness always triggers homesickness.

I walk across the sandy ground toward the Tabernacle. Hundreds of tennis shoe tracks are imprinted in the sand. As I get to the double doors, I look up and to my surprise I see something I never expected to see- there is Seth smiling as he enters the Tabernacle. His parents have brought him back for the evening service. We visit and laugh.

Then Molly hits me with a bombshell, "Seth brought his clothes to stay." I start to protest. The visions of a midnight phone call, complete with Seth crying in the background, whirls in my mind. But Seth is determined to try it. He's switching cabins to where there is a counselor from his hometown. He grins and runs off to join the rest of the boys.

Some stories have happy endings and this is one of them. Every time I see Seth the rest of the week, he is playing and laughing. I'm happily amazed as he happily has a great week. A week that he will always remember and a week of R.A. Camp I can never forget.

Chapter thirty-five

One of the Best Nights of My Life

I pull into the camp at 10:00 P.M. Normally I would be going home at this time, but tonight my night is just beginning. Sitting in his white GMC truck, John Bohacek waits for me. John, or "Mr. Bo" as he is called, is one of the directors at Boys Village, a boy's home near Lake Charles. He is one of my favorite people- a big burly ex-McNeese football player and one of the sweetest Christian men I know. It is a pleasure to work with him throughout the summer as boys from their ministry come to Dry Creek.

But I feel no pleasure tonight. It is the third night of R.A. Camp for Boys. John and I are leaving now to go bring one of his boys out of the woods. Ben (not his real name) is a sixteen-year-old Boys Village resident who is camping out in Kisatchie National Forest with our older outdoor group. He has been ordered to report to another facility by 7:30 tomorrow morning. No manner of pleading by me can put it off. So John and I are going to the Wild Azalea Trail to get Ben.

We leave in John's truck and begin to visit as we drive down the deserted country highway. John is so fresh in his love for Jesus and the boys he works with. I tell myself that although I'm dog tired, this is going to be a good trip. We laugh and exchange stories as we travel northeastward toward Alexandria.

But there is no laughing as John tells Ben's story. I'll not go into it but it is a lifelong sad tale of abuse, neglect, and hardship. Soon our hour and a half trip is over and John's headlights shine on the gate at the Gardner fire tower- our trail head.

Now begins the interesting part of our journey. Two

miles of walking on the trail to the campsite on Valentine Creek await us. I've walked this part of the trail numerous times but never at night. We turn on our flashlights and head out. Being in the woods at night is completely different from the daylight. Everything looks different and sinister.

As we walk, we pray out loud for Ben. We pray for his salvation and the opportunity for him to know a new start with Jesus Christ in his life.

The trail is clear and the walking is easy. We simply follow the footpath and marks on the trees. For every turn in the trail, I have a story about previous hikes on the Wild Azalea Trail, and John listens patiently.

After about an hour, we begin approaching the creek. The trail winds downward and the trees change from pines to hardwoods. It is now after midnight and I expect we'll surprise a sleeping camp of thirty-five boys. But soon we hear voices of campers visiting and see the dim fires of several campfires.

It is at this point that John and I devise our plan. As we get nearer to the camp site, which is across the creek, I begin hooting like an owl. The happy banter around the fires stops as a voice says, "What was that?" Once again, I softly hoot the eight noted call of the Barred Owl.

The boys are quiet now. Silence is only broken by the noise of rustling leaves as boys move closer to the fire. Finally a camper tentatively calls out, "Whhhoooo's out there?" John applies the coup de grace. In his loud ex-coaches' voice he booms out:

"Park rangers, show us your permit."

All kinds of shuffling, rustling, and whispering occur. Many of the boys shine flashlights toward us but we're carefully hidden behind a beech tree thirty yards away. Then I hear the sound I was waiting to hear.

An authoritative adult voice booms out from inside a tent,

114

"Hey boys, what's going on out there? Be quiet!"
One of the boys answers back,
"Bro. Fred, there's a park ranger out there."
You will best enjoy the rest of this story if you know Rev. Fred Hartzell, First Sergeant (U.S. Army Retired). Fred, a wonderful pastor and friend, is the director of the outdoor camp. Our outdoor camp is run with military precision and the firm leadership of a retired platoon leader.

I hear Fred quickly unzipping his tent as he booms out in his best Ft. Polk drill voice,
"Who's out there?"
John matches him leather lung for leather lung with,

"Park ranger, sir, I need to see your permits."

Even though I'm across the creek hiding in the bushes, I can read Fred's mind as he thinks, "Permits? Since when did you have to have permits to camp in Kisatchie National Forest?"

By now John and I are walking the notched log over the creek. I nearly fall in- partly because of the darkness and partly because I'm laughing so hard. Several boys meet us at the foot of the log. Then in the dim light of the fire I see Fred striding toward us, flashlight in hand. He is clad only in his underwear and t-shirt, but every step says "I'm in charge here." As he gets to us he asks, "What's going on here about permits." As he says this, he shines the light in my face and stops in mid-sentence.

It is at this moment Fred recognizes me. And it is at this moment I know Bro. Fred doesn't cuss because it would have come out. We all have a good laugh and try to explain the purpose of our midnight visit. Soon all of the boys and counselors gather around us. Herkie McDonald gets his stove out and makes a pot of coffee. We sit around the dying fire

115

listening to the crickets, drinking black coffee, and enjoying the special fellowship that men have out in the woods.

Finally we must get Ben and go. He loads his pack up. It is a special moment as he tells his Boys Village friends goodbye. No one says it, but they all sense they won't ever see each other again. The three of us walk back across the log and leave to the echoes of good-natured joking from the boys.

On our walk out, we take our time. John shares with Ben what he knows about his situation and move. As John talks, he finds an opportunity to share about Ben's need for being born again. John asks him, *"If you died would you go to Heaven?"*

"No"

"Why not?"

"Because I've been a pretty bad sinner and don't deserve to get in."

John then explains how all of us are sinners and do not deserve to enter Heaven. He relates how Jesus has provided the way into God's presence.

John asks, *"Ben, would you like to invite Jesus into your life?"*

"No, I'm not ready to give up my old life."

We walk on in silence for a while. I simply try to share with him that he may not always have the opportunity to accept Jesus. Life is so unsure for all of us, especially a teen living out in his kind of world. I relate about how suddenly Brad's life ended and how none of us are promised tomorrow.

The three of us walk on in the darkness. As Ben asks John many questions, I sense a melting of his heart. I am just walking silently and praying as we go. When we finally get to the truck, I climb into the back seat. John cranks up the truck to run the air conditioner. One last time he says to Ben, *"Would you like to ask Jesus into your heart?"* Ben quietly answers, *"Yes, I would."*

John tells Ben to simply talk to God about this. After a time of silence, he haltingly begins to pray. Initially his praying is about what a good day it has been and thankfulness for "Mr. Bo." In my mind I'm thinking, "I don't believe he understands."

Then Ben simply says, *"Jesus, I've been a pretty bad sinner and don't deserve to go to Heaven to be with you. But I'm asking you to save and forgive me and come live in my heart. And Jesus, I want to thank you for saving me now."*

I look up and see the dashboard clock blurrily reading 1:18 A.M.. The blur is partly from the late hours but mostly from the tears in my eyes. It will always live in my heart as a special moment.

The trip home was quick. John and Ben talked a great deal. I snoozed off and on. We pulled into the camp gate just at 3:00. It was late but there was time for one more good prank. As we turned in, our faithful night director, Gary Hahler, came out of the dark with his flashlight trained on John's truck. I quickly ducked behind the seat and told John, "Get him."

Gary, who is a pastor and local schoolteacher, dutifully came over to John's door and said,

"Sir, can I help you?"

"I'm here looking for Curt Iles."

Gary said, *"Well sir, he's home in bed. Can I help you?"*

John, in a dramatic graveled voice intoned,

"Well, I'm from the sheriff's department with a warrant for his arrest."

Gary responded with horror,

"An arrest warrant for Curt Iles! What in the world for?"

(From my hiding place in the back seat, I could see Gary's mouth hanging open. I bet his mind was already spinning wondering what kind of trouble I'd got myself into.)

"I'm here to arrest him for overcrowding the camp."

Gary immediately knew he'd been had. We all had one more good laugh (mainly John and I) before saying our goodbyes.

As I got into my truck to go home I looked around the quiet camp grounds. I thought to myself, "This has got to be the most unpredictable job in the world. I'm glad I don't have a boring job. Unpredictability- it's the best, and worst, part of my job."

As I drove out the gates going home for a few hours of sleep before the last day of R.A. Camp, I said out loud, "Tonight had to be one of the best nights of my life . . . "

Chapter thirty-six

At the E.R.

The local emergency room is a place every camp manager dreads to go. Many times my perfect day is interrupted with a call on the radio, "Bro. Curt, this is Nurse Judy. I need to see you in the First Aid building."

When I hear that, I know there is a good chance, we are going to Beauregard Memorial Hospital twenty-five miles away in DeRidder. Normally, it's just a couple of stitches. Sometimes it is a possible fracture. No matter how careful we are, with more than twelve thousand people per year coming to play, swim, canoe, climb, run, and be together, accidents will happen.

And my trips to the E.R. often allow me to get to know campers better. My first trip as manager was during R.A. Camp in 1993. Aaron Stanley, a R.A. camper from Singer, got clobbered on the back swing with a putter. Our trip together to DeRidder resulted in four stitches and a lasting friendship. Aaron is now an older teenager. When I see him at camp, it is always a pleasure to see how he has grown.

But as I stand in the emergency room on Tuesday, July 20, I'm not here for stitches or x-rays. I've followed an ambulance into town carrying Mr. Bill Harrod. During the drive here, the realization has hit me that Mr. Bill is dead, probably the victim of a heart attack. They had called me on the radio for an emergency in dorm 4. The boys there couldn't rouse Mr. Bill for breakfast. We did all we could do until the paramedics arrived. The hardest part was then going out to his campers sitting in the pavilion. Their stares told me more than any words could tell. I'm sure my look conveyed to them the seriousness of this.

I had enjoyed watching Mr. Bill and his boys from

119

Fullerton Baptist Church on Monday. During the evening service they stood in the back of the Tabernacle singing and following the motions to the songs. Mr. Bill, who was a robust man, stood tall above his group of nine through twelve year olds.

But now these boys all sit quietly on the pews in the pavilion. Andy, their staff counselor points out Eric to me. He is Mr. Bill's grandson. I don't know what to say to Eric, but just hug him up and sit by him. If there is anything I've learned this summer it is that words are inadequate but just being there is priceless.

And inadequacy is what I feel now as I stand in the E.R. waiting room with Judy, Mr. Bill's wife. The shock of this sudden event permeates the entire room where many of his family members have gathered. I don't know what to say to this sweet woman whose world has just crashed down. So I simply say the words we can always share, "I care and I'm praying for you."

There was a time in my life when I said, "Well, all I can do is pray for you." But God has taught me that praying for folks in times of tribulation is the most important thing we can do. I recently read a quotation attributed to Vance Havener:

"We often think prayer is preparation for the main thing. But we need to learn that prayer is the main thing."

Eric, the grandson, sits quietly in the Emergency room. There is just something special about this young man that even this sad time cannot hide. He has a shy smile and a kindness about him that both my wife, DeDe, and I notice immediately.

Finally, when there is nothing more to do, I leave to go back to the camp. A heaviness and complete exhaustion hangs over me. On the drive home, I recall a quote by Mother Theresa,

"I know God will not put on me more than I can bear. I just wish He didn't trust me so much."

I know God gives us grace to handle whatever comes our way. God has proven Himself faithful in this manner over and over again this summer. However, I'm beginning to wonder what's next . . .

I return to camp to deal with the many issues that have come up with on this sad day. We are so blessed with how everyone pitches in and helps. Dr. Sam Williams, a Christian psychologist from Lake Charles, cancels his afternoon appointments to come be with our campers and counselors. We see campers open to the gospel because of the day's events. As always, Romans 8:28 proves true as God weaves victory through the events of today.

The next day as I walk down the camp road, there is Eric. He comes up to me with the special, quiet smile he has. Without my asking, he says, "I decided to come back to camp. It's what my grandpa would have wanted me to do."

With that said, he turns and runs off to join dorm 4 on some activity. And Eric leaves me to stand and ponder the wonderful grace of God. How He stands by us not just during the joys of life, but holds us close during the trials and troubles that come to us all.

"For all things work together for those who love God..."

-Romans 8:28

Chapter thirty-seven

Uncle Buddy

I've always loved missionaries. Those who serve God away from home have always been my heroes. I first began this love of missions as a young R.A. boy. Throughout my years of camp at Dry Creek the yearly act of being with real live missionaries has only deepened my respect for these folks.

This summer, as always, we were blessed with great missionaries. But one missionary who really stood out was Buddy Wood. "Uncle Buddy" as he was called by the campers, is a retired Southern Baptist missionary who served in Africa and Asia. He brought many of his African items of interest- zebra skin, machete, snake skins . . .

Bro. Buddy related to me how since being widowed several years ago, he had poured his life into sharing missions at camps like Dry Creek. It was evident from when he arrived that here was a man passionate about sharing the vision of foreign missions . . .

He set up this display in the corner of the new snack shack. Throughout the day he spent hours with the kids sharing about missions. His time in the Tabernacle with the campers was well-planned and received. As I sat and listened, I wondered how many future missionaries might be in this crowd. Or how many, like me as a pre-teener, would develop a lifelong love and respect for missions through a camp experience.

As I sat there my mind drifted back to the R.A. Camps of my boyhood. For more than ten consecutive years there was only one camp missionary- Dr. Kenneth Trent. Dr. Trent, pastor of Second Baptist Church in Channelview, Texas, was the perfect missionary for boys.

Now Dr. Trent wasn't a true missionary in the literal sense. His mission stories came from yearly short-term trips to Africa or South America. Kenneth Trent was a great storyteller and showman. He understood that young boys were impressionable and would be spellbound by stories that told of the native countries and the sharing of the gospel.

As Dr. Trent held up an African Tribal machete and told of the warriors coming to his messages holding menacely onto their machetes and spears, I felt as if I were there. He would wave the machete wickedly as he shared a story relayed by one of the career missionaries of warriors coming to kill members at church only to be turned back by the power of prayer.

He would then hold up his Masaai blood gourd and tell in gross detail of how the tribal members would mix cow urine, milk, and blood for their daily lunch while in the bush with the cattle. When he'd describe the drink, I could nearly taste it in my mouth.

I heard these stories year after year but always looked forward to them. And the stories were simply a vehicle to do what Dr. Trent really wanted to do- share the gospel of Jesus Christ.

On Wednesday night of camp he would show slides of his mission travels. Invariably he would end the program with a beautiful jungle sunset. Dr. Trent would plead that for many in the world "The sun is going down without them knowing Jesus Christ." He would always issue an invitation to any boy who hadn't accepted Jesus Christ. Turning to point at the red sunset he would remind all of us that this could be our last sunset to make life's most important decision. Many a young man made life-changing decisions during those services. Ricky Gallien, one of my boyhood friends, was saved during such an invitation. Ricky now serves as pastor of Calvary Baptist Church near Merryville.

Even though the African "curios," as Dr. Trent called his display items, were popular, nothing could match two South American items he had.

The first was a stuffed piranha fish. This fish, about the size of a man's hand, sported needle-sharp teeth. Dr. Trent described in graphic detail what would happen to a cow or pig that wandered into a piranha-infested stream in the Amazon. Even swimming in Bundick Creek was scary after the piranha stories.

But the ultimate curio he had was saved until the last day of camp. Dr. Trent would pull a small glass box out of a paper bag. Inside the glass box was a genuine shrunken head from Ecuador. I'm not sure how he procured it but it was real. You've never seen the attention of three hundred boys riveted on anything like the shrunken head.

It was about the size of a man's fist. Dr. Trent would explain the native process of shrinking a head. Once again this conversation piece, and what a conversation piece it was among the boys, was only a tool to share the gospel. Dr. Trent would share how this man, killed by an enemy, had never heard the gospel. The need to share Jesus everywhere was once again burned into my heart.

I still encounter men of my age group who after finding out I work at Dry Creek say, "When I attended camp as a boy, there was this missionary with a shrunken head. Do you remember him?" I smile and reply, "How could anyone forget Dr. Kenneth Trent."

So as Uncle Buddy unwraps another item from Zimbawae and ten- year-old boys ooh and aah, I know that new lifelong love of missions is being born in hearts at Dry Creek.

Chapter thirty-eight

Will it Last?

It's a full house in the tabernacle tonight. Our Back to school youth camp always is an exciting week. Campers and adults just show up expecting God to work. And He has worked in a mighty way this week.

Because of the many campers and the large number of guests, we've moved chairs into the Tabernacle. Tonight I'm sitting on the front row- a place I seldom sit.

The camp pastor, Troy Terrell, begins his message. All eyes and ears are on him as he paces the stage sharing a passionate story about obedience and commitment to Jesus. About twenty minutes into the message a young man get up from the middle section of the Tabernacle. He catches my eye just as he gets to the front.

Let me describe this camper. He looks to be about seventeen. He is a big ol' boy- about 5'10" and a good 240. He doesn't hurry as he comes forward- he just sort of ambles. Looking at him I know he is country and I mean that as a compliment. He just looks solid . . . and I'm not just talking about his physique.

I think to myself, "He's coming up to pray at the altar." But he bypasses the pews that serve as our prayer area. He slowly comes up to the steps in the middle of the stage. All eyes are on him . . . even Bro. Troy has stopped in mid-sentence.

My next thought is, "He is going to hit the preacher!" But the slight smile on big boy's face tells me differently. Then the thought hits me that he is going to share an impromptu testimony.

But he ambles by Troy and the microphone to the edge of the stage. Into a white trash bag on the stage he puts an object from his hand. The bag has been on stage all week. During the week, teens have placed items that they wanted out of their lives. I had peeked into earlier and saw shattered musical C.D.'s, magazines, even a wadded pack of cigarettes.

I have a pretty good idea of what he had in his hand, but I won't tell you because the object doesn't matter- the act of his heart does. Just as slowly as big boy came, he returns to his seat. As he passes Troy, he simply nods his head in the way country men do as a sign of respect.

I breathe a sigh of relief that he didn't sock Troy or disrupt the service. Then I realize what a beautiful act of obedience we'd witnessed. We adults may feel led to give up something in repentance, but few of us would go up front during the middle of a service. We'd wait until the Tabernacle was empty and discreetly go to the white bag.

But that's what I love about young people. They passionately act on their feelings toward God. They practice something we can all learn from- Instant obedience. Instant obedience is something all of us so-called mature Christians should learn about. If God lays something on your heart, do it and do it now.

Bro. Troy now gets his second wind and is preaching full speed ahead. But my mind is still on the sermon I've just seen. Then the thought creeps into my mind: I just wonder if he'll be keeping his commitment two months from now at school. In other words, "Will it last?"

Quickly I feel Holy Spirit conviction on my attitude. I recall where I've been reading in Luke about the lost sheep. In Luke 15 Jesus says,

"And there will be greater rejoicing in Heaven over one sinner who repents than over ninety-nine other righteous men who need no repentance.

The thought hits me: There's no one in Heaven right now

saying "Will it last?" They are just rejoicing. And if they are rejoicing, so should we.

And then I think back to a young man in this same building in 1972. During the youth service God has spoken to many young people. Some have come forward to be saved. Others just like our big boy this summer have stepped forward to get some junk out of their lives. Others have come just with a desire to follow Jesus closer.

During this service nearly thirty years ago, one young man simply comes to the front to pray. The desire of his teen age heart is be surrendered completely to do whatever vocationally God wants Him to do. There is nothing sensational or even emotional about his decision. He is simply offering a blank check to God to be filled in as He wishes.

I'm sure someone thought, "I wonder if it'll last?" Because of God's faithfulness, that decision has stuck. Here's how I know that- I was that young sixteen year old boy.

I've not always been what I should be but as I've sought God's will each step of the way, God has graciously led me step by step. Never in my wildest imagination did I dream that my prayer at the front of the Tabernacle would lead me to leading this camp one day.

I hope in future times as I have the continued privilege of watching God work in young lives I will not become calloused or cynical of seeing young people make commitments. Our encouragement and support are what teens need as they make decisions to follow Jesus in a full way. What a privilege we have to be there for them.

Chapter thirty-nine

Tabernacle Prayer

Dear Lord, as I sit in the back of this old building called "the Tabernacle" at Dry Creek.

I'm reminded of all the great things you've done in this building.

Above the loudness of youth singing

And the echoes of sermons from your word,

I can hear your sweet, still, small voice above all the other things I've heard.

As I look up at those exposed rafters, I sure do wish they could talk . . .

All the stories they'd tell of lives changed here by You...

Souls changed by the power of your love never to be the same again . . .

Missionaries and Pastors who first heard your call, "Go and tell . . . "

While worshiping in this building.

Lord, thank you for using this camp and the Tabernacle on these grounds

To speak to thousands of lives over the years.

But Lord your power isn't confined to any building,

For your Spirit works everywhere.

You're ready to use people and buildings, when we're simply open to your will.

But I'm surely thankful you've chosen to work in such a mighty way at Dry Creek.

Thank you for all the marvelous things you've done here in the past . . .

But most of all Lord, thank you for what you will continue to do at your camp.

As we plan and look to the future, lead us as we plan,
Let everything we do, be guided by your strong hand.
And let my life be Your tabernacle,
A place where You're welcome to dwell,
Always remembering that without Your presence
No building, or person, is complete. Amen

Chapter forty

Brothers

There they stand on top of the power pole- Luke and Rory Haynie. As they stand on top of the 30-foot high pole, their arms are around each other as they prepare to jump. I'm down on the ground holding one of their safety ropes. It is truly a Kodak moment because of how special these two guys are.

I first met Luke Haynie in March. He was sitting waiting for me outside the student center at Louisiana College. I was to interview him for a summer counselor's position. He sat there on a bench- a big strong boy with a baseball cap and an easy smile. I walked up to him and spoke. He smiled and said, "You're Curt Iles from Dry Creek, aren't you?"

I said, "No, I'm Bill Smith, I'm here selling insurance." Luke Haynie looked at me suspiciously and then I burst out laughing. There on that bench I began my love affair with this unique young man.

The next time I saw Luke was at our Spring Preteen Retreat. He had an unusual haircut which explained why he had the ball cap on two weeks earlier. His hair was highlighted in the style that many teens prefer- streaks of blonde washed in.

But as Luke counseled the pre-teeners in that spring weekend, it is not his hair I notice- it's his big heart. He is naturally friendly, kind, and lots of fun. We are excited to hire him for the summer.

When he shows up in June he has changed his hairstyle- it's even more radical than before. I have trouble in writing explaining visual images, but let me try- I call it a "porcupine haircut." His high-lighted hair is combed back and sticks up in little tiny spikes.

In the mornings when Luke comes in his hair often looks as if his finger was in a light switch. It sticks up all over. . . But Luke has my heart. He is a great counselor and a favorite of everyone. He wears a nametag that says, "My name in Luke. Ask me about Jesus." He loves sharing his faith and does in a creative cutting edge way.

The only morning I can't take the hair is the first morning of Boys Opportunity Camp. Luke has spiked it up with mousse. His hair stands up in about eight vertical spikes. He looks like the Statue of Liberty. I do a poor job of explaining how this style will be a distraction to the boys. Luke obediently, but reluctantly, goes back to the dorm and combs it down.

Week after week Luke is used by God in cabin 2. On the weekends he goes to several of our country churches to preach. I'd like to be a bug on the wall when he went in with that hair. I can just see those redneck men when they first see Luke's hair. However, I hear good reports from each church on what a blessing he is.

As we near the end of the summer, Luke asks me if his brother, Rory, can be squeezed into Back to School Youth Camp. Luke is burdened about some poor decisions Rory has made recently and feels that a week at camp is just what his younger brother needs. Luke prays fervently with me about his brother's spiritual needs.

Rory's mom brings him over from Carthage, Texas on the second day of camp. Now Rory doesn't have porcupine hair. He has dyed his dark hair blonde. It is a unique style just as bizarre in its own way as Luke's. We place Rory in Luke's cabin. As I observe throughout the week, it is evident he is having a great time.

On Thursday afternoon is when these two brothers come to the Power pole. This event on our outdoor challenge course is the ultimate event. It is a scary event that will shake the knees of the stoutest camper. A thirty foot high pole with climbing staples leading up. The top is a small platform just big enough for two people to stand on. A trapeze is suspended seven feet out front. The object is for both partners to simultaneously jump together to catch the trapeze bar.

Now it goes without saying that the jumpers are hooked to safety harnesses manned by us on the ground. But when you are standing on a swaying pole, thirty feet in the air, no harness or rope gives you enough security. The power pole has another name- "The pamper pole." I bet you can easily figure out how it got its name!

How special it was to see Luke and Rory up there together. Luke had climbed first and then helped Rory up. It was a wonderful picture of the encouragement Luke had given his brother spiritually.

So arm in arm they stand there. They are talking in each other's ears. I'd like to hear what they are saying. Then they yell out "1...2. . .3. . . jump!" and with a hoarse scream they launch out together to the trapeze.

...God does a real fresh work in Rory's life during this week of youth camp. At the end of the week, Luke comes to me, "Bro. Curt, would it be possible for Rory to stay next week and help me as a counselor in cabin 2?" When I looked in Luke's eyes, I knew it would be wrong to say no.

So our last week of camp, Luke and Rory were together as Preteen counselors. Once again I was astounded that when God gets in control of a person's life, dramatic changes occur. Rory was not the same guy who'd arrived last week. There was a light in his eyes and purpose in what he did.

On the last night of services, I slip into the gym where campers are being counseled on personal decisions they've made. I call this area the "spiritual maternity ward." Sometimes when I lose focus on what camp is about; I go back to the gym to watch new birth taking place.

And tonight is no exception. All over the gym in chairs and on pews, counselors are listening to campers. But it's over on the ping pong table my attention is riveted. There sitting with a camper are Luke and Rory, one on each side. They are sharing the gospel.

And suddenly it doesn't matter to me that one has porcupine hair and the other is a peroxide blonde. All I see are two brothers... Two brothers who've found the common bond that holds brothers together- the love of Jesus Christ.

Chapter forty-one

F. Scott Fitzgerald

One song will forever link my mind with the summer of 1999. The song is the "Charlie Brown theme song." This is the song Schroeder is always plinking away at on Charlie Brown T.V. specials. Here's why this song is still playing in my mind.

On the first day of camp when our counselors arrived, Scott Fitzgerald walked to the piano, sat down, and began playing the few notes he knew of the Charlie Brown song. And I'm not exaggerating when I said "few notes." It was obvious Scott had many talents but playing the piano for our services was not going to be one of them.

Let me describe Scott. He is a big strong McNeese student with an easygoing smile and quiet manner. He still looks like the football player he was in high school. In addition Scott is very nice-looking. During G.A. Camp for girls he was the resident heartthrob.

In his cabin, Scott handled all of his campers well. He especially showed a gift for working with troubled kids. I quickly grew to appreciate Scott and his low-key but confident leadership style.

When camp started, Scott would grace us at each meal with a concerto of his entire repertoire- The Charlie Brown theme song. Amazingly, he didn't neglect his campers to play- they were all gathered around him as he exhibited his skill. But I'm not sure I initially grew to appreciate Scott's piano playing. At first it got on my nerves. But soon I began to appreciate his perseverance.

Eventually I did notice that he was picking up a few notes and showing more rhythm in his playing. He told us, "By the end of the summer, I'm going to know this song."

On weekends he would play the song over and over. Fellow counselor Davy Funderburk, who is a wonderful pianist, began working with him. By July 4th, Scott was now playing his one song with both hands. As I sat eating my eighty-first hamburger of the summer I thought to myself, "He's going to get it." The fact that he had marked his strategic keys with colored tape didn't take away from the miracle I was hearing.

What I began to notice now was how Scott had two passions in life: being a great counselor and playing Charlie Brown. He was extremely focused on these two and these alone. As I watched and listened God reminded me of the value of persistence. Just sticking with a task and daily doing your best will result in success. God wants faithful servants who will simply play the notes they've been given the best they can.

Because Scott was faithful to his song, great improvement began to show by July. You could hear the hundreds of times he'd practiced coming out in the music. Anytime he went to the piano, several staffers would gather around to encourage him and help him.

As the final week of camp started, Scott made an announcement that he was planning to play his song at our end of the summer party.

For the next few days I didn't hear Scott playing as much in the Dining Hall. On the night of our party at Roy's Catfish Hut in Kinder, we transported the camp electric piano in a van. Scott had carefully marked the keys with tape. He sat down and put his music on the music stand. It was the score for this song. We all laughed because we knew Scott didn't know a note from a link of boudin.

But then he launched into his song. It was stunning. Someone had taught him a little classical introduction. He'd been practicing privately the last few days and had added

135

several other twists to the song. It was played with a fast tempo and very well.

But most of all it was played with a deep passion. I've heard many musicians play but I'm not sure I've ever heard anyone play with more passion and deep expression. The song came from F. Scott Fitzgerald's heart. He finished with a flourish. All sixty of us burst into spontaneous cheering. My wife, DeDe, who was a piano major, whispered, "That was something else!"

It was something else! And the reason it was so special was because Scott Fitzgerald had the perseverance and persistence to stick with his dream.

Chapter forty-two

Godly Sorrow Brings True Repentance

When I arrived, an eleven-year-old camper named Luke stood by the camp golf cart. I'd been summoned from the cafeteria after being told "A camper had driven the golf cart into the side of the Tabernacle."

Walking over I expected to find glass and broken wood everywhere but instead there was a little scratch on the cart and a single tile broken on the Tabernacle wall. The boys who had reported the crime all pointed at Luke who stood there looking at me defiantly.

As quickly as I could, I scattered the onlookers and kept only the few eyewitnesses. All manner of accusations and counter-suits began flying around as to who had hatched the plot, pushed the cart, and actually been behind the wheel during the dirty deed. I finally hushed the boys down. At this point I thought the best justice would have been to have taken off my belt and wore all of them out. But I wisely decided against that course of action.

As I cross-examined the participants, the truth began to emerge in a quilted patchwork of lies and half-truths liberally mixed with the actual truth. It was evident Luke had been the captain of the ship when the golf cart took off. Apparently he had put it in reverse and backed up before turning the knob to forward and running into the Tabernacle wall. When confronted with this, Luke stood up to me and vehemently defended himself: "I wasn't even near here." Then, "It was another boy who looked like me." I looked at camp director Billy Ray Franks and wearily shook my head. This was going to be a tough nut to crack.

But finally Luke began to soften.

"Well, I was on the golf cart, but I didn't mean to hit the

wall."

And finally the truth, and nothing but the truth, came out.

"Yes sir, I was driving the cart. I took off backwards and then sped forward before hitting the wall."

Then I asked the question I'd been waiting to spring, "Luke are you sorry you did this, or just sorry you got caught?"

He pondered my question for a moment before quietly answering, "I'm sorry I did it. It was wrong of me to be on the cart in the first place."

...And my mind went back to one of my favorite camp stories. The late sixties and seventies were an interesting time in summer camps. The youthful rebellion of the sixties had finally hit rural Louisiana and the battle had begun. All authority seemed to be in question- even at camp. Redneck boys, who had two years earlier sported flat tops, now had shoulder length hair and muttonchop sideburns. Girls tried to show their rebellion with miniskirts were shorter than they needed to be.

The generation of this time had to test every limit. One of the ways camp authority was tested was boys trying to slip out of the cabin at night. Routinely boys would slip out a window of the old dorms and roam around. The night watchman at this time, Walter Mahaffey, would tell me all kinds of tales about chasing boys in the darkness. I remember a camper from Shreveport who came into breakfast with a crease mark across his forehead. He related how he had been out when the night watchman hollered at him. As he ran, he encountered a clothesline that was sagging just a little (or maybe he was a little too tall.) The result was the mark he had.

Now here is my story from 1970: Two local teens at camp were caught outside by the night watchman. The next day the camp director, a pastor, gave them this option- They were to be sent home unless they would apologize to the entire camp for their misdeed.

I'm sure the guys contemplated this option. They sure wanted to stay at camp. But the idea of getting up in front of all of their friends and two hundred female admirers to apologize was a bitter pill to swallow. But nevertheless they agreed.

That night at the service there was a huge crowd (The Tabernacle and gym were not divided at this time.) Both boys were introduced by the camp director, and then they nervously came to the microphone. After coughing the first boy said,

"I'm very sorry I was outside in the dark last night. It was wrong and I want to ask you to forgive me."

The auditorium exploded into hand clapping mixed with cries of "You're forgiven!"

The pastors and youth leaders in the audience nodded their heads in approval and the smiling camp director put an arm around boy #1's shoulder.

Now it was the turn of boy #2. He stepped up much more confidently. I thought to myself, "Just repeat what he said and you'll be fine." But no, he had worked out his own speech and here it is:

"Well, I'm sorry I was out last night. But most of all, I'm sorry I got caught."

There was an eerie silence in the Tabernacle. No one knew what to say or do. In my fourteen-year old mind, I wondered, was that apology or wasn't it?" But there was no doubt what it was in the mind of the now frowning camp director. He roughly grabbed boy #2 by the arm and unceremoniously led him from the stage. As they went out the side door, he was giving the boy an earful.

And that story of nearly thirty years ago was my first

139

introduction to the difference between Godly repentance and worldly sorrow. You see, true repentance from God is sorry for the sin. A repentant person wants to change directions, make amends, and do right- regardless of whether they got caught or the waiting consequences.

However, worldly sorrow simply is sad it got caught. It's already thinking, "Next time I'll be more careful or crafty." The sorrow of the world doesn't change a person.

But I'm so thankful Godly sorrow does change a person. Repentance simply means to change directions from the path we were on. It is a 180-degree variation.

And as I stood outside the Tabernacle with Luke, I was ready to see if he meant business. "Luke, there are three things you must do now to show you are truly sorry. First of all, I want you to apologize to Bro. Reggie Hanberry for bothering his golf cart. Secondly, you'll owe ten dollars for the damage done. Finally, you'll have to go with me now and sweep the Tabernacle.

Luke who fifteen minutes earlier was ready to fight a buzz saw, meekly agreed to the consequences. And as he, Billy Ray, and I swept the Tabernacle, I've never seen anyone do a better job of sweeping under every pew and in every corner.

For Godly sorrow produces repentance leading to salvation, not to be regretted; but the sorrow of the world produces death.

II Corinthians 7:10

Chapter forty-three

What it means to be sold out

Often we talk about the mission of Dry Creek Baptist Camp being the three S's:

People being saved, sold out, and sent out.

-Saved means meeting Jesus personally as Lord and Savior.

-Sold out means letting nothing stand in the way of following Jesus.

-Sent out means God's long time way of calling out Christian leaders.

I want to share about the most dramatic instance of a young person being sold out

I've ever seen. It began last summer in Brad Robinson's life. As I've shared from earlier stories Brad came to us and really worked hard and won us all over.

All summer long it was very evident how he was growing in the Lord. There was a fire and boldness for Jesus that Brad couldn't hide... and he didn't try to.

When he returned home to Hicks, Louisiana, this fire continued. Brad exhibited a passion for sharing with his friends. He'd made a commitment to stand up for Jesus, and he intended on following through with it.

When his basketball coach made a comment to Brad, "You've got to choose between basketball and God," Brad quickly made that decision. He gave up a sport that was very dear to him and his family. I always wished he had stuck with the team and proved a point to the coach about commitment to Jesus. But I couldn't argue that Brad had shown where his allegiance was.

On September 12, 1998, we had our annual See You at the Pole Youth Rally at Dry Creek. During this event, Brad

141

felt God calling him to the preaching ministry.

Sometimes in September I received an E-mail from Jessica Midkiff, Brad's youth leader.

She shared how their whole youth group and school had been affected by Brad's new found commitment. It warmed my heart to hear how God was using Brad in his school.

Because Brad's church youth consisted of three schools-Hicks, Pitkin, and Oak Hill High, The revival began to spread to these schools too. In addition, Brad had a big influence at nearby Simpson High School. Because Brad was such a social person, he seemed to know every teen in every one of these schools.

Throughout the early part of 1999 Brad continued to show the fruits of a sold out Christian. All he wanted to talk about was Jesus. Well, let me correct myself- He still was girl crazy and sports-minded, but even these subjects took a backseat to his walk with the Lord.

His websites and E-mail were tools to share his faith. (You can still check him out at bloodwashed@bigfoot.com.) The plan of salvation was shared on his home page.

During the spring Brad began getting opportunities to preach in area churches. God was opening all kinds of doors for him.

As I think about this shining example of being sold out, the parable of Jesus about the growing seed in Mark 4:26-29 comes to my mind. Christian author T.W. Hunt shared that this is the most overlooked of Jesus' parables. It states:

This is what the kingdom of God is like. A man scatters seed on the ground. Night and day, whether he sleeps or gets up, the seed sprouts and grows, though he does not know how. All by itself the soil produces grain- first the stalk, then the head, then the full kernel in the head. As soon as the grain is ripe, he puts the sickle to it, because the harvest has come.

T.W. Hunt then added, "Salvation in a person's life is an instanteous event. Becoming like Jesus is a lifelong growing process. That is what occurred in Brad's life. Jesus grew the seed into a great harvest of lives.

So often in camp we get excited about the "Road to Damascus" experiences where the worst teen in camp repents and turns his life to Christ. These 180 degree experiences are worthy of our rejoicing. But I never want to overlook the "5 degree" course corrections that God begins in the hearts of youth.

They say to turn a large ship is a series of 5 degree nudges of the rudder. I once read in our Christian Camping International Journal, that some of the greatest camp decisions are the first of those "small" course changes that God begins in a precious life.

That's what happened to Brad. I don't believe there was one moment or day in the summer of 1998 when he became sold out. I believe it was a process that God began. And when God begins something He is pretty good at continuing it... as He proved in Brad's life.

As you are probably aware, Brad's earthly life ended on Saturday, June 26, 1999.

He was killed in an automobile accident near his home when struck by a drunken driver.

I often go by his grave at Mt. Moriah cemetery. He's not there, but it gives me some comfort to just visit. On his vault is a Dry Creek bumper sticker that states:

Where Jesus is Changing Lives.

. . . If ever that motto was true, it was true in the life of Brad Robinson.

Soon they'll erect his marker. It'll say May 10, 1982-June 26, 1999. But I wonder if that last date is really correct.

Because some time last year, during the summer of 1999 the old Brad Robinson died... and the new sold out Brad Robinson let Jesus take over.

Brad Robinson heard, and acted on the words of Jesus in Matthew 16:24-25:

If anyone would come after me, he must deny himself and take up his cross and follow me. For whoever wants to save his life will lose it, but whoever loses his life for me will find it.

While with us, Brad gave us many gifts. For me he gave the gift of what God can do through a sold out teen willing to make a stand. The words of D.L. Moody echoes in my mind,

"The world has yet to see what God can do through a person completely sold out to God."

Now Brad wasn't perfect but his life did show what God can do with a burning fire in a person's heart. And even his death has not extinguished the harvest resulting from the seeds planted by a sold out teenager named Brad.

But Brad didn't just give us special gifts while with us. He left us a lot of notes that have blessed us. Brad's ten year old sister, Brittney, shared this with me. The week after Brad's death Brittney asked God for some assurance of Brad being with Him in Heaven. While rummaging through Brad's desk she found this poem written in Brad's handwriting:

Streets of Gold...a crystal sea.
With the one who died for me.
There I'll live for eternity,
With the ones who asked to be set free.
He paid the price for all to see,

He gave His love unconditionally.
The streets of Gold, a huge crystal sea
Mansions as far as the eye can see
No more pain, tears, or strife
Just me and Christ for all time.

Chapter forty-four

The Swamp

It's Wednesday morning as we all sit or stand in the Swamp all twenty five of us. Now the Swamp is a classic building at Dry Creek. It is the summer home of our boy staffers. I recall with fondness the summer twenty years ago I spent in it as staff director. To all of us guys who've worked at camp, there is a special brotherhood from sharing a summer here together.

But today it's not just guys in the Swamp. Our whole staff is gathered here. This loud group, whom you normally can't shut up, are all silent. As I sit against the wall, I stare at a dime on the floor. I'm the fearless leader of this group and I don't have a clue what to say.

You see it's the last week of camp and we've all left our responsibilities trash runs, floor sweeping, washing dishes, and all the other behind-the-scene jobs we do daily to gather at the Swamp to load up Brad's stuff.

It's been five weeks since Brad died. We've left his bed and gear as it was on the day he left to go home that fateful weekend. His parents told us to keep it there until the end of the summer. . . And now that time has come. We've all come summer staffers, counselors, and those of us who work here year round to say another good bye and close another chapter.

All week long I've become emotional just thinking about this moment. To me personally it has such an air of finality to it. The last visible links we have to Brad Robinson will be loaded up in a few minutes to make their final journey home.

I continue to stare at the dime on the floor right by Brad's bed. I wonder how long it has been there and what story it could tell. We all sit in quietness except for the air conditioner and many sniffles. After what seem like hours, but in reality are only minutes, I finally say, "Guys, you're going to have to do it."

Then our staff boys slowly, but resolutely, begin what must be done. They unplug Brad's stereo and pick up the C.D. collection he loved so much. They open his closet and bring out his clothes. His hats his faithful Yankees cap and camouflage basket hat. come next. One by one with the love and care I've seen soldiers fold the American flag, they fold and box up Brad's stuff.

As I sit against the wall in the corner, the tears just seem to pour out of me as a torrent broken forth in a flash flood. I don't know where it is all coming from. It's not coming from just my eyes but from my soul. All of the pent up emotions I've carried in my heart just burst through. I put my head in my hands and just lose control. The pain of loss, the broken dreams of Brad's future, the sorrow of closing this chapter and saying good bye one more time, seeing Brad's friends weeping are just too much for all of us. The room is filled with sobbing as we all grieve together.

When I finally look up through my tears, the boys are folding Brad's quilt and picking up the extra mattress he depended on for a good night's sleep. Finally everything is loaded in the big blue storage box.

Just as we all sit there, no one wanting to take the first step to the door, five camp radios blast out. The voice of Doris Hennington loudly calls, "Diaaaannnnne." It is Doris's famous panic call. At once all of us in the Swamp burst out in uncontrollable laughter. Just when we needed it, the Lord sent just what we needed. As we all laugh heartily with the tears all mixed with humor and sorrow I know we're going to be all right.

The boys load Brad's stuff in the back of my truck. Mixed with his gear is potting soil and mulch to plant a tree at Brad's house when they get there. I walk by the truck and touch for one final time Brad's storage box. Once again I'm walking by his coffin seeing his face for the last time this side of Heaven. Once again I softly say, "It's not good bye, Brad but see you later. . ."

Chapter forty-five

A Good Epitaph to Have. . .

Have you ever thought about what epitaph you'd like to have? Last weekend, as I walked along the seawall in Galveston, I saw one I admired. A plaque there read:

In memory of Leroy Columbo 1905 1974

A deaf mute who risked his own life repeatedly to save more than one thousand lives from drowning in the waters surrounding Galveston Island.

As I looked out over the Gulf of Mexico, I wondered about what kind of man Leroy Columbo was. Evidently here was a man who exhibited a passion for saving lives. I suspect he was a man who overcame his physical challenges, and put everything fiber of his being into the life saving business. As I gazed down the beach, I could nearly see Leroy Columbo sitting alertly on his lifeguard stand. There he was the most focused lifeguard on Galveston Island. I can picture him sitting on his perch oblivious to the surrounding honking horns and squealing children. His focused gaze surveyed the waters for the signs of a swimmer in distress. . .

I can imagine his joy as he handed a rescued child over to a terrified mother- how many lives and families were changed by his live saving work! With each saving act, his passion grew deeper to do what he was born to do save lives.

As I stood there, I thought about the job of Dry Creek Baptist Camp. Our reason to exist is to be a place where Jesus rescues souls in need of God's grace. That is to be our focus and passion. Just as Leroy Columbo did, our focus and concentration must be on the job God has called Dry Creek to do: being an environment where God's presence is felt and lives are changed.

As we see what God has done this summer we are so thankful. We cannot change one single life only God can touch lives as we've seen. All of the over three hundred fifty salvations this summer are God's work not ours. Whether it is a seven year old asking Jesus into her tender heart, a rebellious teen repenting and turning to God, a high school senior surrendering to missions, or an adult counselor making a decision to be a better parent, lives are changed by God at Dry Creek.

I'm convinced that now is one of the most important times for presenting the gospel to today's generation of young people. Never has there been a greater need. . . or a better opportunity. Youth today are not satisfied with worldly things and are sincerely searching for what we know is the answer a personal relationship with God.

. . .And those of us who serve in Dry Creek's ministry, especially those of you who labor by praying faithfully, are a key part of what God is doing.

Let's keep our gaze out on the waters as we strive to reach those who need the life changing news of how much God loves them. Let's do whatever it takes to serve and minister to others! What greater privilege is there in life than to be part of a person coming to know Jesus Christ.

Pray often for Dry Creek. . . It's the most important thing you can do!

"In the same way, I tell you, there is rejoicing in the presence of the angels of God over one sinner who repents."

Luke 15:10

Chapter forty-six

The Day the Circus Leaves Town

My two younger sisters and I all worked as summer staffers at Dry Creek. What a blessing to our lives have been the lessons we learned at camp. As our workers often say, "It's the hardest job you'll ever love." The long hours, dirty chores, and low pay are nothing compared to the special experience of being part of a great team of teens working together for God's glory.

The closeness a group of staffers experience gets during the summer is hard to describe. It reminds me of Louis Armstrong's answer to the question, "What is jazz?" Armstrong replied, "If I have to describe it to you, you haven't heard it." Summer staffing cannot be described- it must be experienced.

When summer ends and the staffers go home, a strange silence settles over the camp. Even though we'll be busy on the weekends, nothing can replicate the excitement of summer camp and the part our teenage staffers play in it.

The adjustment for our staffers is also tough. They go home fatigued from a great summer of feeling every emotion possible. They take home with them pictures, dirty clothes, their cherished poster signed by every worker, their foot washing towel, and a heart full of love and memories. They must re-adjust to being at home again and returning to the real world of school.

It is to this adjustment time that I now refer to. My sister, Colleen, two years younger than I, loved being a staffer as much as anyone. One summer she came home from a wonderful summer of staffing. She collapsed wearily on the couch as she looked down at her now calloused hands. Her summer staff boyfriend was gone back home. Her many camp friends had scattered to the four winds. She sat teary-eyed and exhausted, staring out the window.

My dad, always quick with just the right comment, walked through the living room and silently observed Colleen sniffling and pouting on the couch. He simply commented, more to all of us, than Sister Colleen:

"It sure is a sad day when the circus leaves town."

How many years since then have I applied that quote to the end of summer camp. As I walk across the camp today there is a thick silence everywhere. Only an hour ago there were hundreds of happy campers saying goodbye and promising to keep in touch. Now only a piece of paper blowing across the grounds tells of their presence. As I walk to the Tabernacle to shut off the lights, their footprints in the sand are the only evidence of a week of camp just ending.

The Tabernacle is always the place where the silence is most felt. It reminds me of my coaching years. It was always a special moment to be the last to leave the silent gym after an exciting game was over. In the now darkened gym, my footsteps echoed across the wooden floor in stark contrast to the cheering crowd that was here not an hour ago.

The Tabernacle is now completely empty. The only noise is a squeaking out of balance ceiling fan. For just a moment I sit down. It's hard to gather all of the deep feelings I've felt this summer- the countless victories, the hilarious events, the lives that've rubbed up against mine and enriched me, even the sorrows and disappointments of this summer. I walk outside. It is now growing dark. The sunset across ball field number one is beautiful. My favorite night sound at Dry Creek- the crickets in the trees are now singing their nightly song. My final thought of this special summer is,

"The summer is over...Long live the summer."

Chapter forty-seven

Shining Your Light on Friday Night

One of the things I enjoy most about camp are the seasons. What I'm talking about are the different paces and types of events each time of the year bring. Of course there is nothing like the summer camp season. It's like being a scared cowboy riding on a raging bronc. You know you're overmatched but you're in the saddle anyway. You want to get off but you're too scared to let go, so you ride it to the end. But I love summer and summer camp. Even now as I rest in the shadow of summer 1999, I'm looking ahead with anticipation to next summer.

With the end of summer camps, we return to retreat season. Dry Creek goes from a busy weekday place to primarily a weekend destination. We love the number one question asked of us, "When summer's over, what do y'all do?" I used to try to explain it but I gave up long ago.

Because retreat season is special in its own unique way. And there is nothing like Friday nights. This is the time most weekend groups arrive. We have a saying at Dry Creek:

"When Friday evening gets here, the clock means nothing."

No one arrives when they say they will. Groups of fifty planning to eat at 6:30 P.M. arrive at 8:13 with thirty-two people. Then there are the many unexpected requests and changes that occur when you have several groups staying in different facilities and sharing a dining hall.

I'm afraid I sound as if I'm complaining- I'm not. I love it! There is a great rush to seeing excited youth come driving up in three church vans followed by eight carloads of senior adult ladies from another church. You know it's going to be fun introducing each group to each other at supper.

153

There is a momentum that builds with Friday evening. An anticipation that God is going to do some good things among our guests.

I had that feeling tonight as the men from Another Chance Ministries ate supper. Their fifty men sat and enjoyed fried chicken and good fellowship. The beautiful sound of forks clinking, laughter, and the buzz of conversation is what I call "the sound of fellowship taking place." It is the foundation of the spiritual victories that will be won later in the weekend.

As I look at this group of men and boys, my heart is warmed. This group, from one of our black churches, has come yearly for the last three years. It is always good to see old friends. If I were to independently ask our staff, "Name your five favorite groups we have each year" I would daresay all of our workers would include at least three black groups among their five. Our African-American friends are so special. They have taught me so much about worship and just how to enjoy the camp setting. They love to help out-many will not leave the dining hall until we've let them wipe the tables. There is a sweetness about these church groups that ministers to me way more than I can minister to them. I sense and feel the spirit of Jesus among them.

Another Chance Ministries has requested a campfire at 8:45 P.M. Because it is Friday I think, "Well, they'll probably actually start after nine." At 8:30 I get my Friday night tools- a BBQ pit lighter and flashlight and ride my bike to the Prayer garden.

As I ride my bike through the pines, the night breeze feels cool after a scorching August day. I'm thinking of the quiet time I'll enjoy at the Prayer garden as I await our guests. But as I ride past the Lodge I'm dismayed to find them marching out of the Lodge, in formal procession, on their way to the campfire.

The only problem is that the camp fire doesn't exist-yet. I've got fifteen torches to light and then get the actual fire going. As I pedal furiously, I pass the lodge and arrive at the first torch. Fifty yards behind me are the singing men marching slowly across the pine straw carpeted road. Passionately and in unison they sing:

"Gonna lay down my burden . . . Give it to Jesus
Yes, lay down my buurrrrrden... Give it to Jesusssss."

I feel pretty good about it now as I ditch my bike and pull the striker from my pocket. I'll just go on quickly and light the torches. By the time they get to the Prayer Garden, I'll have the fire going good. I light the first three torches and maintain my fifty-yard lead. Behind me I still hear,

"Gonna lay down my burden . . . Give it to Jesus."

The singing is beautiful. The rich acapella voices of these men echo through the woods. Sound always carries better at night and tonight is no exception. Many of the men are adding parts and additions to this wonderful song about giving our problems to the Lord.

But I don't have time to stand and enjoy the singing because they are gaining on me. And it's precisely at the fourth torch when my burden becomes heavy. The striker I'm using to light the torches doesn't strike. Only a tiny spark emits where a flame should be. I feel sweat break out on my forehead as I repeatedly click the striker. Eventually on about the fortieth click I get this torch lit.

The only problem is my delay has brought the singing procession of men much closer. I don't have to look back; I can hear the singing much closer now:

"When I get up to Heaven . . . give my burden to Jesus
Gonna lay down my burden, give it to Jesus."

I decide a new course of action. I'll skip every other torch. Hopefully they'll still have enough light to get down the trail. But lighting any torch is a chore. Hardly any sparks come from the striker and I'm left in the dark with my frustration and regret for not bringing a backup.

I finally get to the bridge. I must light the torch at the bridge so the men can see their way across. To my joy, the torch lights quickly. I'm glad because the footsteps of the singing men are right behind me. I scurry across the bridge and jog to the camp fire.

I pour diesel on the wood and pull my trusty striker out. Over and over I click it to no avail. The men are seated now and one of them begins a beautiful prayer that all of the others join in agreement on. I slip to the side bench and whisper for a cigarette lighter. One is passed to me. I go to the fire and light it. As always, I burn my fingers holding the lighter long enough to the wood to catch. But by now pain means nothing. We are going to have a camp fire no matter what. As the men continue in prayer, I kneel by the fire as it catches and flames up.

It is with profound satisfaction that I pull the impotent red plastic striker from my back pocket and toss it into the fire. I stay just long enough to watch it melt and then I slip away from the fire. I return the cigarette lighter and slink into the darkness. I figure I've quenched the spirit enough tonight and should get out of the way A.S.A.P.

As I recross the bridge I look over at one of my favorite Dry Creek sights- the lit cross reflected in the pond. This wooden cross, eight foot high, is beautiful to see at night. I've seen it hundreds of times but it always catches my eye and heart. Behind me the men continue in spirit-filled prayer. I stop on the bridge and join in simply praising God for how great He is.

When I go back up the trail, I decide to light the torches

I'd skipped. From the woods I get several pieces of dry pine limbs and dip them in an unlit torch. I go back to the nearest lit torch and carefully take my small fire to the next unlit torch.

As I put the pine limb to the torch and it erupts in light, the men are silent as their prayer has ended. Then a lone baritone voice sings out, quickly joined by others:

This little light of mine, I'm gonna let it shine.
This little light of mine, I'm gonna let it shine
This little light of mine, I'm gonna let it shine,
Let it shine, let it shine, let it shine.

As I head up the trail to my bicycle, I thank God for Friday nights when **His light** shines so brightly.

157

Chapter forty-eight

The Pine Knot Pile...A Lesson on Earthly Treasures

All of a sudden, the February wind picked up and turned out of the south. Instantly, what had been a small controlled fire in my back field became a raging monster.

The flames spread rapidly through the dead knee-high grass . . . As fast as I could, I ran ahead with my faithful fire fighting weapon, a wet grass sack.

But no one person, nor any wet sack, was going to curtail this fire. It seemed to have a mind of its own and malice as it raced northward.

DeDe and the boys came running out of the house. Armed with brooms, buckets, and a shovel, they ran to join me but were also driven back by the raging racing fire.

All five of us knew exactly where the fire was going-right toward one of our most precious possessions-my pine knot pile.

Now before coming back to the fire, let me cue you in on what a pine knot pile is.

Southwestern Louisiana was naturally populated with Yellow Pine, or as we now call it, Long leaf Pine. Every area of upland was covered with these slow-growing but stately pines.

During the late 19th and early 20th centuries, all of the virgin pine forests were clear-cut by large timber companies. Where huge tracts of pines once towered, only open fields of stumps now stood. These companies came in, cleared large areas for miles, and then moved on.

These yellow Pines had many great qualities. Prime among them was the tree's inner core, or heart. This heart, instead of rotting away, turned into a rich, resiny hard wood.

158

These remains of pine stumps, or trunks, were called "fat pine" or "rich lighter."

Due to its thick rosin, lighter pine would burn easily and has always been the preferred method of starting fires in cook stoves and fireplaces for generations.

In the 1940's, Crosby Chemical Company of Picayune, Mississippi moved into Beauregard Parish and began harvesting the remaining stumps for their turpentine mill.

Turpentine is the syrupy liquid in these pine stumps. It is used for many purposes.

Country people gathered all of the rich pine they could for their personal use. Every older home had a large pine pile in the back yard or near the barn. My grandpa had a sled built to pull behind his horse. He could go out into the woods and pile knots and stumps onto his sled.

Every home proudly considered their pine supply a great prize.

Fires were the method of keeping warm and cooking. During winter a fire was usually burning in either the fireplace or cook stove around the clock. However over the years propane and electricity became part of our rural culture, cook stoves and cooking in the fireplace became lost arts.

But most people still kept their fireplaces going. There is no substitute for sitting cozily by a popping and crackling fire as the cold wind and rain blow against the house. And to have a good fire means having good rich lighter pine to start the fire.

When DeDe and I bought our house in Dry Creek in 1985, I was excited to also inherit the huge pine knot pile in the corner of our back field. The land on which he lived had been a second growth forest until it was cleared for soybean farming in the 1960's. This was during a time when the price of soybeans skyrocketed and many people cut and cleared their pine forests to plant beans. Today, it is so ironic that all of these soybean fields are once again pine plantations- the bottom fell out of the soybean market in the late 1970's due to overseas competition.

Anyway, as they cleared the land I now live on, they piled the pine stumps and knots in a huge pile- a pile that reached head high and twenty feet wide.

I inherited this lifetime supply of pine when I purchased our house and the surrounding ten acres. With pride I pointed out this pile to my family and visitors. I could feel the envy of men as they commented on this vast and valuable pile. There was enough here to last a lifetime and more. Starting a fire in our fireplace was easy with the pine splinters cut from these stumps.

I wasn't completely selfish with this abundant supply. I shared wheelbarrow loads with my dad, family, and neighbors. Even after ten years of use, I hadn't even made a good dent in the pine pile.

...But now this fire, started by me, was approaching the pile and was going to make more than a dent in it. As suddenly as the brush fire got to the pine pile, it was all afire. I'll always remember the intense heat as the entire pine pile erupted in flames. The flames and thick black smoke billowed high in the sky.

If it'd been anything but my pine knot pile, it would have been enjoyable to watch...

DeDe went inside and called the fire tower to inform them as to the source of the thick black smoke. Tommy Harper, the tower man, replied to her, "Ma'am, go easy on your husband. It's a tough thing on a man to lose his pine knot pile."

It all happened so quickly and was over in a matter of minutes. There where fifteen minutes earlier my pine knot pile had stood, there were only charred ashes and smoking chunks of wood...

I think back to my precious pine knot pile when I read Jesus' words in Matthew 6. He reminds us that all earthly treasures someday rust, corrode, rot, become moth-eaten, are discarded, or as in my case, burn up.

When you see someone driving a new car off the sales lot, remember that one day the car, now so shiny and new, will be junked, crashed, discarded, and smashed flat to be melted down.

Earthly treasures have their place, but they are only temporary. Just like my pine knot pile, they can so quickly and unexpectedly leave us. But the things of God, the Heavenly treasures- the things that really matter... are eternal and last forever.

Do not store up for yourselves treasures on earth, where moth and rust destroy and where thieves break in and steal. But store up for yourselves treasures in Heaven, where thieves do not break in and steal. For where your treasure is, there your heart will be also.

-Matthew 6:20-21

Chapter forty-nine

Just Keep on Paddling

Greatness is not where we stand, but in what direction we are moving. We must sail sometimes with the wind, and sometimes against it- But sail we must, and not drift, nor lie at anchor.

Oliver Wendell Holmes

Our canoe drifts into the swift cold waters of the White River. All of a sudden we've left the calm waters of the narrow Buffalo River and now we are paddling furiously upstream in a raging much wilder river.

Frank Bogard and I are at the end of a three-day August river float on Arkansas' beautiful Buffalo River. On the secluded last thirty- miles of this designated National River, we've seen no humans but have enjoyed the company of eagles, deer, and beautiful views. It has been a serene and peaceful trip out in God's great creation.

But there is nothing serene or peaceful where we are now. To get to our pull out spot, where our truck is located, we must paddle upstream for one half mile at the point where the smaller Buffalo River enters the White River. Our location on the White River is south of Bull Shoals Lake. We'd been told to make our upstream paddle in the morning. In the morning is when the upstream dam, where electricity is generated, is not releasing water into the river. During the hours of water release, the White River becomes a large and dangerous stream.

Well, we have arrived early in the morning but there is no doubt they are releasing water upstream. The river is high and raging. Right ahead of where we enter the White, a large island extends into the channel. All around it foaming water flows as the river narrows into a raging torrent. Trees are flooded on the opposite bank. Just past our entry point and slightly downstream, the loud noise of water hitting a large rock area catches our attention.

As we come into the White River's strong influence, I'm amazed at how cold the water feels. The bottom of the canoe becomes cold to my sandaled feet. And the cold water, just released hours earlier from deep in the depths of Bull Shoals Lake, has what I'd describe as a cold smell. I zip my life jacket tighter wondering how long a man would last in these ice cold waters.

And then Frank and I do the only thing we can do: We begin paddling as if our life depended on it. For a while I wonder if we will be able to escape the grip of the White River pulling us backwards and downstream. But as we get our bow straight, paddle in unison, and hug the left and, we begin to make progress upstream.

One half mile doesn't sound like much, but paddling a canoe upstream against the current of a mighty river makes it a long distance. We both paddle furiously. Soon sweat pops out on my forehead, in spite of the surrounding cold air and water. There's hardly time for conversation between Frank and I- all of our energies are on one thing- getting upstream away from the raging stream and rocks behind us.

The entire time I hear water crashing into the rocks downstream. I feel that if I stop paddling for even one stroke, that will be enough to lose our momentum and pull us back and into the rocks. My arms ache and burn but I must keep paddling. My whole mind and body are consumed with only one thought: Just keep on paddling.

I also remember that at some point we must paddle across the river to our docking point on the opposite shore. As we continue slow progress up the west bank, we encounter a fishing boat with a man and two boys. Meaning to help us by moving away, they crank their engine and start to move to the side. But the boat is being guided by one of the boys. He comes dangerously toward us and their momentum looks as if they'll capsize us when we collide. I just know we're going into the cold water. Our boats come within inches of each other before they pull away.

Furiously, we begin paddling again, intent on regaining our lost momentum form our encounter with the fishermen. Just as Lot left Sodom without a backwards glance, I tell myself not to look back, only ahead. By glancing to the left, I can tell we are making good headway as the shoreline eases by.

We are now in a straight and wider stretch of the White. And now we know we are going to make it. Seeing the landing, ahead and across the river, we begin angling across the wide river. This area of the river, though wider, doesn't have the same pull of current as it earlier did. Soon we are across and at the landing.

What an experience this entire trip was. I'll never forget the rapids on the Buffalo, seeing a doe and her twin fawns crossing the river as we stood fishing. I'll cherish the bald eagle we saw fly over and the sound of the whip poor wills calling at Elephant Head Bluff as we camped out. But long after I've forgotten these, I believe I'll remember the cold clear water of the White River and our paddling with all of our soul and might to get upstream.

Because already many times since our trip, I've come up against obstacles and difficulties. And each time I've heard a voice deep in my heart imploring me to keep on paddling, don't quit.

And to you my reader, especially those who are in the midst of a tough upstream paddle against the raging troubles of life, Just keep on Paddling. Don't give up.

"Never, never, never, never quit." -Winston Churchill

Chapter fifty

A Loving Hand

The Time is Now

If you are ever going to love, love me now, while I can know
The sweet and tender feelings from which true affection flow.
Love me now, while I am living. Do not wait until I'm gone.
And then have it chiseled in marble, sweet words on ice cold stone.
If you have tender thoughts of me, please tell me now.
If you wait until I am sleeping, never to awaken,
There will be death between us, and I won' hear you then.
So if you love me, even a little bit, let me know it while I am living.
So I can treasure it.   -Author unknown

I sit in the Alzheimer's ward at Westwood Manor. I'm in town on the first day of a week's vacation after nine weeks of summer camp.

But here at the nursing home it is not vacation time. Instead it is lunch time and the residents are sitting down to eat. Many stare blankly into space, and others are fed by aides. There sitting with her back to the wall, with her eternal smile, is the lady I've come to see- Mrs. Corinne. As I sit down beside her, she lovingly grips my hand. As I look down it is such a stark contrast to see my dark tanned hand next to her pale, white, weathered hand.

Her hand, now holding so tightly to mine, is nearly

transparent. I believe if I put a light underneath her hand, the light would shine through. It reminds me of my precious grandmother's hand just before she died. In fact Mrs. Corinne reminds me so much of my Grandma Pearl. That's one of the reasons she is one of my favorites.

Her hand is so fragile looking- weathered and covered with age spots. As the nurse brings her plate of dumplings, greens, and cornbread, I laughingly tell her, "Don't tell Mrs. Corinne's husband that her boyfriend is here holding her hand." We all have a good laugh at that.

As she clings tightly to my hand, we visit. She is one of the sweetest ladies I know. She and her husband, Mr. Jay, have always been special friends with five generations of my family. People like Mrs. Corinne and Mr. Jay are some of the last links to the old Dry Creek I heard about from my great grandparents.

As I look down at her loving hand on mine, I'm reminded of a few years ago when I saw Mrs. Corinne's hand gripped in Mr. Jay's at their 60th wedding anniversary. What a special day that was at the White House, our Adult Center at the Camp. Here they were celebrating a lifetime together in the building where they attended school as children.

But as I've learned, time marches on . . . and Alzheimer's waits for no one. And so here we sit in the nursing home. I think about how bravely Mr. Jay has handled this... and how tough a decision he was forced to make to bring his sweet wife here.

I think about my precious wife, DeDe, and how we've just celebrated twenty years of marriage. And I realize that if God gives us enough years together, one of us will probably have to take care of the other... and make some hard decisions.

And once again, as I stand at the end of a wonderful and terrible summer, I'm reminded of the greatest truth I will take with me from summer 1999- Life is a wonderful, precious, and fragile gift. Each day, each moment, each opportunity to love, is like the wonderful fragrance from the wild honeysuckle in the spring.

Between my house and the camp, on the bank of Mill Bayou, is a honeysuckle tree that is the earliest bloomer in our area. Each March I watch it carefully each time I drive by. When it blooms with its pink fragrant flowers, I love to stop by and smell the blossoms. To do so, I must climb the barbed wire fence and dodge through a minefield of cow patties and then get my feet muddy to go down to the creek bank. But the work is worth it all. There is nothing like the first scent of honeysuckle after a long cold winter.

There are times when I've seen my favorite honeysuckle and put off going to visit it. I've been too busy or just decided to come later... and then suddenly I would look out as I drove by and realize this year's blooms were gone. A late frost, or my hurriedness, had cost me.

And as I look down one last time at Mrs. Corinne's hand, I know to leave; I will have to forcibly pull my hand from her grip. I'm once again reminded how we need to inhale each moment deeply, because life and those we love passes by so quickly. And how if we have something good to say to those we love, say it now. Don't put off one important thing because life goes by so swiftly...

This is the beginning of a new day.
God has given me this day to use as I will.
I can waste it or use it for good.
What I do today is important because I'm exchanging a
day of my life for it.
When tomorrow comes, this day will be gone forever:
Leaving something I have traded for it.
I want it to be gain, not loss. Good not evil.
In order that I shall not regret the price paid for it.

-Zig Ziglar

So as we end this time spent together on the creek bank, my parting words would be the from the story above... Soak in the love of God and your family. Enjoy the wonderful gift of friends, walk among the trees and hear God's whisper in the wind among the pines.

...Take time to sit on the creek bank and watch the water flow by.

Curt Iles

About The Author

Curt Iles lives in Dry Creek, Louisiana with his wife DeDe. They are the parents of three grown sons.

A former teacher, school principal, and camp manager, Iles is now a full-time writer and speaker. He is the author of four books: Stories from the Creekbank (2000) The Old House (2002) Wind in the Pines (2004) and Hearts across the Water (2005).

His latest book, The Mockingbird's Song, will be released in early 2007.

To learn more about Curt Iles and the ministry of Creekbank Stories, visit www.creekbank.net.